Unexpected Journey

By
Joost R. von Weiler

Order this book online at www.trafford.com
or email orders@trafford.com

Most Trafford titles are also available at major online book retailers.

Note for Librarians: A cataloguing record for this book is available from Library
and Archives Canada at www.collectionscanada.ca/amicus/index-e.html

Printed in Victoria, BC, Canada.

ISBN: 978-1-4269-0157-7 (Soft)

*We at Trafford believe that it is the responsibility of us all, as both individuals
and corporations, to make choices that are environmentally and socially sound.
You, in turn, are supporting this responsible conduct each time you purchase a
Trafford book, or make use of our publishing services. To find out how you are
helping, please visit www.trafford.com/responsiblepublishing.html*

*Our mission is to efficiently provide the world's finest, most comprehensive
book publishing service, enabling every author to experience success.
To find out how to publish your book, your way, and have it available
worldwide, visit us online at www.trafford.com*

Trafford rev. 6/4/2009

Trafford
PUBLISHING® www.trafford.com

North America & international
toll-free: 1 888 232 4444 (USA & Canada)
phone: 250 383 6864 ♦ fax: 250 383 6804 ♦ email: info@trafford.com

The United Kingdom & Europe
phone: +44 (0)1865 487 395 ♦ local rate: 0845 230 9601
facsimile: +44 (0)1865 481 507 ♦ email: info.uk@trafford.com

10 9 8 7 6 5 4 3 2 1

Contents

FOR LYDIE,
THE PERFECT TRAVELLER''S COMPANION

THE ROAD NOT TAKEN
Robert Frost, American poet
(1874-1963)

Two roads diverged in a yellow wood,
And sorry I could not travel both
And be one traveler, long I stood
And looked down one as far as I could
To where it bent in the undergrowth;

Then took the other, as just as fair
And having perhaps the better claim
Because it was grassy and wanted wear;
Though as for that the passing there
Had worn them really about the same,

And both that morning equally lay
In leaves no step had trodden black.
Oh, I kept the first for another day!
Yet knowing how way leads on the way,
I doubted if I should ever come back.

I shall be telling this with a sigh
Somewhere ages and ages hence:
Two roads diverged in a wood and I-
I took the one less traveled by,
And that has made all the difference.

Chapter One

The Family, The Early Years

Our family has its roots in the Duchy of Gulik, West Germany. In various documents in government archives in Dusseldorf, a Gerhardt von Wilre is mentioned in 1163 and other family members, an Alexander de Wilre in 1217 and a Thoenis von Wilre, also spelled von Wylre. It was not until Jakob von Wilre von der Lohe appeared on the scene, that we began to have proper records. He lived from 1491-1555 and his last name indicated that he lived on an estate, called Loherhof, near Uetterach in the Parish of Dremmen. He bought the estate in 1545 from the widow Nopperney and her two sons, and there he brought up his family. In the family crest, wine grapes are featured and it is presumed that the Loherhof had vineyards like most estates in the region. Jakob's grandson later became a wine merchant in the city of Sittard in Limburg province in Holland. Through the ages, family members were either professional people or merchants and sometimes the merchants in the family became rich.

The head of the branch in Berlin, for instance, Leonhard, who was born in 1549 became a banker and a merchant.We know little about his father Heinrich other than, that he lived in Gulik, had a high position at the Court of Justice and was married to Martha Zuhr. His only son, Leonhard was born in 1549. The family owned a country estate, where they farmed. They probably had a tenant on their farm to do the actual work. Leonhard was not too interested in this activity, and decided early on, to move out of his parental home to seek his fortunes in Berlin. He probably got the idea from the sons of his uncle Nicolaus, who left for Berlin earlier. Leonhard was interested in trade and commerce, which was a big change for a boy from the country. In the second half of the 16th century big trading houses sprung up in Berlin and young Leonhard soon found a job, which was a junior position with the trading house of Jobst Krappe and it was there, that he started his incredible career. Jobst Krappe was wealthy and influential, but it was Katharina, his daughter, who was hotly persued by young Leonhard. It was not long after he arrived at the scene, that he married Katharina Krappe and was offered a full partnership with the firm. Jobst Krappe and his wife Eva Doring also came from the Gulik area and seemed to take a liking to Leonhard, whose career was about to take off.

Trading in those days was a risky business. With so many wars going on all the times, the company was selling cloth for military uniforms, gunpowder, leather articles, such as boots, muskets, weaponry and other needed articles to warring parties. The company was official Purveyor to His Majesty at the Court of Chur-Brandenburg, but the buyer was not always able to pay. The company became a bank, as well, and fortunes were lent to pay for the goods. It has been known, that the Bank side of the trading company actually paid for the Thirty Year's War. Sometimes the Chur-Brandenburg court borrowed money from other sources, and the company was always there to guarantee and co-sign the loans. The borrowers were often slow in paying back their loans, and sometimes, the loans had to be written off for non-payment. This was probably regarded as the risk of doing business, but in spite of this, the fortunes of the company and its owners soared.

In 1638 a plague hit the area and Leonhard's son Christian and his brother in law Peter Engel died. The head of a branch of the company died as well and this caused havoc within the leadership of the company, reducing the company's fortunes somewhat. The younger generation of the family took positions with the government. When Leonhard married Katharina Krappe in 1583, he did not know that his father in law, Jobst Krappe had only two years to live. He died in 1585. Being a full partner in the firm brought Leonhard a lot of money and after Jobst Krappe's death, when he took charge of the firm, he was able to bring the fortunes of the firm to great heights. Leonhard now was a very influencial man in Berlin, in fact he was first appointed to City Council in 1585, then he was elected Mayor in 1596, re-elected in 1598 and again in 1600. He died in office a year later. During his career, he was always looking for bright members of the family to join the firm. One bright young man was Jakob Weiler, who was the oldest son of Uncle Nicolaus.

Jakob had studied economics at the University of Straatsburg and saw this opportunity right away. When Leonhard died in 1601 at the young age of 52, Jakob became head of the firm. In 1607, he married Leonhard's widow, Katharine Krappe. She died in 1619 and Jakob did not have any children by her. Jakob re-married Maria Fritze, daughter of a Senator at the Court of Chur-Brandenburg. They had three sons and three daughters and all we know is that the youngest daughter Sophie (1627-1701) later married the Mayor of Spandau. After Leonhard's death, the firm changed its name to Jakob Weiler and Leonhard Weiler and Heirs. Jakob died on July 6, 1626. He was 57 years old. His widow re-married to a bookkeeper in the firm, who was at his job for twelve years, when all of a sudden his fortunes changed for the better and became a full partner. During the Second World War, the Allies bombed the City and one bomb destroyed the Nicolai Church in which Leonhard was buried.

Leonhard and Katharina had five children: Katharina, Justus, Maria, Christian and Ursula. Of the two sons, the oldest, Justis, decided to take a government job. He was born in Berlin in 1585 and studied at the Universities of Wittenburg, Leipzig and Heidelberg. After his studies, he traveled all over England, France and Italy and on his return to Berlin he was offered the job as Secretary of the Chancery of the Chur-Brandenburg Court. He married twice, first to Margarethe Schonbeck (1596-1625) the daughter of the Mayor of Standhal, who died in childbirth, and two years later to Sara Stowe. His brother Christian was a partner in the Weiler's Trading Company and Bank in 1619; the company changed its name to reflect the fact, which it was now in the hands of the von Weiler family. Jakob was now head of the firm. Other family members in the firm included his sister Ursula and his brother in law, Tilman Eisenbruck, who was the brother in law of Jobst Krappe. The owners of the company were always on the lookout for opportunities and they acquired a large interest in the silk and textile-manufacturing firm of Sturm und Eisenbruck in Cologne-am-Spree. The individual partners in the firm all bought large estates. Peter Engel bought a very large one with a mansion called Reinickendorf. He paid 10,000 thaler for this property, which he bought from the City of Berlin. Christian bought three estates and mansions, Cremmen, Vehlefanz and Staffelde and his heirs lived there until the 18th century. He bought these properties from the bankrupt estate of the von Bredow family. It is strange, that Lydie and I made friends with Henning von Bredow and his wife Jane in Toronto. Henning settled in Canada in the fifties, just like we did.

While the von Weilers made fortunes, they also donated large sums of money to charitable institutions. They built a library for the Maria church and built a gymnasium in a convent. Even during the war years of 1616-1648 they built a large senior citizens complex for retired clergymen, their widows and orphans. In the end, this branch of the family died out due to lack of male heirs. The company slowly lost its golden touch and eventually was disbanded. The Rothchild-like fortunes of the 16th century von Weilers were lost and the story ends in 1784 when the Berlin branch of the family ceased to exist.

This was the time during which the big war was fought on German territory. It involved most major powers and the conflict was initially between Protestants and Catholics. The rivalry was between the Habsburg dynasty and other powers. Catholic France chose the Protestant side, increasing that rivalry. The impact was famine and disease. While this war lasted for thirty years, the conflicts that started it all lasted longer. The war ended with the treaty of Westphalia. Countries involved were Sweden, Bohemia, Denmark-Norway, the Dutch Republic, France, Scotland, England, Saxony, the Holy Roman Empire, Spain, Austria and Bavaria. The military taking part at the time consisted of 150,000 Swedes, 75,000 Dutch, 100,000 Germans, 150,000 French, 300,000 Spanish and 100-200,000 Germans.

The family in Germany did not produce many heirs and when Jacob Lambert Wilhelm Carl von Weiler was born in Wesel in 1788, he was to start the healthy branch of the family in the Netherlands, while gradually the German branch died out. Jacob studied law at the universities of Heidelberg and Duisburg, and started his career as a lawyer in Wesel and later in Kleef. When he married Wilhelmina Haesbart, the daughter of another lawyer, he bought a small estate called Poelwijk in the town of Out Seventer. This town was at the border of Germany and the Netherlands, and on May 31st, 1815, the two countries, corrected a part of the border and signed an agreement; and the Poelwijk estate became part of the Netherlands. In fact, the whole town became Dutch while further south of the country, a section of the border became German.

Jacob became a Dutch citizen because of the new agreement and acquired his new citizenship. His change of status caused him to lose his German title, but in 1818, he was elevated to the peerage by the Dutch government. Jacob and his wife had many children; four daughters and five sons and they in turn produced forty-five grandchildren for them. One son, Arnold Carl, was my great-grandfather. He had eight children, one of which was my grandfather.

The Poelwijk estate changed hands many times from one family to another, because every time one family owned the estate, the family died out and became in the hands of female members of the family, who married and thus the estate came into the hands of another family. It happened first in 1607, with Lucretia van der Hoeven and the estate came into the van der Hoeven family. This process went on for five and a half centuries during the existence of the estate. Sometimes it was sold as well, as was in the case in 1729 when it was sold to Louisa Catharina de Coenen for 3,000 Dutch florins. This family sold the estate again for 17,600 thaler in 1749. The estate was eventually bought by the von Weiler family in 1783 when it was bought for 42,525 Dutch guilders by Johan Laurens von Weiler, who left it to his son Joan Bartholomeus Gotfried von Weiler and his wife Johanna Frederika Louise Lamers-von Weiler. That was in 1789 and his father made the condition that the estate could not be sold or divided during his father's lifetime. There was a mortgage on the estate, held by Catharina Louisa Charlotte Ten Berg von Weiler, which was paid out in 1807.

Jacob Lambert von Weiler tot Poelwijk was born in 1788 in Wesel, and he was burgomaster of Zevenaar. He inherited the estate in 1835 from his parents. He had several children of which the oldest Wilhelmina Louisa was born on the estate in 1813. His fourth son Gotfried Carl von Weiler tot Poelwijk was a lawyer in Zutphen. Out of this marriage with Sophia van Eck, was born Frederick Eduard von Weiler tot Poelwijk, who married Isabella Anna Mock. Out of this marriage was born Caroline von Weiler tot Poelwijk who married another lawyer, Jacobus Coops. She held on to the estate for years, although she did not live there anymore. At present only the estate's farmhouse exists. When Caroline lived there after the death of her husband, the family still owned an oak pew with an oak canopy in the little church in Zevenaar.

It was custom in those days, that prominent families in town had their own pew with a canopy, and decorated with the family crest on top. In addition, the town council had a similar pew for its members, decorated on top with the crest of the town. The church council decided one day, that it was now necessary to buy these pews from their owners, because they did not like the idea that part of the furniture in the church did not belong to it and now they asked the families and the town council to sell their properties to the church, hopefully for a nominal sum. All owners agreed except one.

Widow Caroline von Weiler gave her answer: a decided "NO". The von Weiler family owned the pew and it was to stay that way. The church fathers discussed this dilemma. One of the members suggested giving his son a chance to act as a lawyer for the first time in his career, merely months after he became one. This young man went to Mrs. von Weiler and repeated the request of the church fathers, and his 'client' said that she made her decision, and that she was not going to change her mind. "I'm so sorry to hear that, Mrs. von Weiler, because now I have to do what they told me to do, if the answer was still no." Mrs. von Weiler was puzzled by his remark. Then the young lawyer told her that he had to take the pew structure apart, and place it on the sidewalk for Monday's garbage pick up. Now Mrs. von Weiler relented and the pew was sold to the church. Now anyone, visiting the church, which is still in service, can sit in one of those beautiful pews, close a little door and then look at the oak ceiling of this beautiful piece of furniture, now owned by the church. Now the family had new roots and slowly, with more male heirs arriving on the scene, the family survived extinction and new blood was nurturing the next generations.

Chapter Two

Between Two Wars

The first world war was still on, when Arnold and Isabella van Styrum were married. It was 1916 and they rented a house in Utrecht. His father asked him what we wanted to be, when he grew up and the answer was short and decisive: a doctor. "Nonsense", my grandfather said, you are good at mathematics and you will become an engineer." And since father knew best in those days, he entered the University in Delft to study engineering. After his studies he wrote his thesis, as required, and his one was on steam locomotives. It was ironic, because in the same year, the National railways changed over to Diesel and Electric. His sister Jep was married to a successful manufacturer of silver products, jewelry and flatware of all descriptions.

Carel Begeer was also a designer of note and designed the special products his company was famous for. Begeer also had a department, which produced art medals made out of bronze and silver, and he needed someone with artistic talent and that was my father Arnold. In the meantime Ies was busy making preparations for the arrival of their first-born. Their first child was a daughter, who was named Florentine, but they used the name Flory. When she was two years old, a son was born, who was called Jacob, or Jaap. The silver company merged with another company in the same field in 1925 and the factory was moved to a town called Voorschoten, not far from Leiden. They moved to Leiden, where I was born. They lived on one of the canals, in an old house, with a large garden. In the garden were a large nut tree and an antique teahouse, where the children played. Flory and Jaap were both at the elementary school, while their father Arnold left every day for the factory. Next door they made friends with Professor van Ronkel and his wife. He was a professor in Arabic languages at the university. My parents enjoyed the company of their neighbours very much.

One day, Arnold and Ies decided to move closer to the factory and they rented a house in Wassenaar, a town close-by. Here, Rudolf was born. Now with three boys and a girl, mother Ies had her hands full. She did have a hobby, however. She was a wizard with needle and thread and that talent came in handy during the Second World War years. She also embroidered tablecloths. Arnold would first make a design on transparent paper, and then she would transfer the design to the linen. She also made lace, an art she learned when she was in Brussels, during her school years, where she attended a French school. Brussels is the capital of Belgium and famous for Belgian lace. Ies was a crack hockey player in her youth as well. Her granddaughter, Sophie, one of Jaap's daughters, who would become an Olympic medallist in the 1980's, would later inherit this talent.

Ies took courses in craft and took lessons on how to sculpt in wood. Once she carved a lion's head from a block of wood. When the carving was finished, her teacher took it off the workbench. On the back was a hole, into which fitted a pin that held the carving onto the workbench, while she carved. The teacher took a piece of paper, wrote a message and put it in the hole. Then he took a piece of doweling and glued it in the hole, to fill the cavity. For year's, I wanted to know what was written on that piece of paper. Jaap, who inherited the lion's head, refused to drill out the hole. "It's much more fun, not to know and to guess", he always said.

Rudolf was born in Wassenaar in 1928. Flory, meanwhile was in secondary school, and one summer, when the rest of the family went off to the World Exhibition in Brussels and after traveling to Luxemburg, Flory went to Switzerland to learn French. It was 1935 and the plans were to make a trip to Luxemburg after the fair. I marvelled at the exotic pavilions and Rudolf and I became separated from our parents. We found a shelter for lost children and waited for hours before we were again picked up by our parents, by then we loved all the playthings so much, we did not really want to go with them. Rudolf and I loved to climb the rocks in the Ardennes and to visit a real castle, the Dillenburg.

One night we drove around and around a mountain. I watched the moon from the back window and was intrigued, because at once the moon was on my left and then again on the right. At the top of the mountain, we saw a brick archway and in a small niche a statue. A man was standing on a ladder clipping the vines around the statue and after he moved, we drove through the archway to the castle behind. Slosz Roth was operated as a hotel and we stayed there for a week. Often Rudolf and I went down to the river Uhr at the bottom of the mountain and our father taught us to skip flat stones over the water. He was very good at it. We wore rubber slippers provided by the hotel, because the river was filled with gravel.

Years later, when Lydie and I were traveling throughout Europe, we were nearby and we walked up the mountain. I was puzzled, when we had to go through a border gate. The castle was just within Germany, and not in Luxemburg, something I never realized. The vines were gone and the niche was empty, but behind we found the castle still intact. Even with the red and white coloured blinds. It was a great experience for a nine year old. While we were in Luxemburg and Germany, Flory was off to Switzerland to learn French. She was nine years older than I, and eighteen. She stayed with the family of a clergyman and after several weeks, she went to England where she stayed with a family at Henley-on-Thames, to study English. She wanted to stay two weeks in Germany to brush up on her German as well, and she went to stay with a family in Berlin. The man of the house was a Rotarian, a service club to which Arnold belonged, but the visit was a disaster. Flory did not like the people and left earlier than she planned.

After her studies, she started a three-year nurse's course and just before the war, she obtained her diploma. At the beginning of the war she started her career at the University hospital in Leiden. In 1943 the Germans were all over the country looking for students to work in German labour camps. They were looking for Jaap as well. Flory was engaged to a young doctor, Jo Bok in Rotterdam. His father was a brilliant brain surgeon, who wanted all his sons to become physicians. When Jo heard about the Germans looking for students and other single, young people to work in Germany, he came immediately to Wassenaar. Flory was indeed in danger as long as she was unmarried. They decided to get married.

Jaap, who had moved with his parents to Leiden shortly after his birth in 1919, finished high school in 1940. At his exam, one examiner asked him what he had read in English and Jaap replied: "All of the works of Shakespeare". They did not believe him and they started to ask questions to test his knowledge. He answered every question correctly. And when he was asked about Hamlet, he recited one piece with a Scottish accent, which obviously resulted in high marks. "How is it that you know so much about Shakespeare?" they asked. "I visited Edinburgh, took in a summer Shakespeare Festival and saw all of his plays" he answered.

Jaap went to Leiden University to study law. This course was mainly directed to the jurisprudence in the Netherlands Indies and since the colony was to become a republic after the war, he was never able to use what he had studied. He did well with his studies however until the Germans closed the university in 1943. One professor, who taught theology in Leiden preached every Sunday in a large church. Behind the pulpit, he had a little suitcase handy so that he could flee when chased by the Germans. He was preaching sermons, which could be dangerous. His name was Professor Cleveringa, and when he was warned that the Germans were after him, he went in hiding. After the war Jaap married Mathilde Gunning and they set sail for Singapore where he was offered a job with a company producing rattan furniture. After three years they returned. Til could not bear the heat and they were looking for a cooler environment.

On their return to Holland, it was still hard to find a place to live and they moved into the house of our parents in Wassenaar. With two children, it was a busy year for our mother Ies. When Jaap was offered a job with a large pharmaceutical company called Organon, the family moved to 'sHertogenbosch, an eight hundred year old city, where they bought a house. Jaap worked for the company for many years, traveling in all the countries in Eastern Europe, Russia, Hungary, and many others. His knowledge of languages was his greatest asset there, picking up more in the countries he visited. He sold pharmaceuticals and sometimes had to take items such as old-fashioned ladies' shoes as barter. He was given gifts by the people he stayed with and had to smuggle these gifts home.

Those adventures were nothing compared to his escapades during the war. He was a member of an underground group, mainly consisting of students. They were smuggling Jewish families into France, where the French students of a similar group took over. They smuggled the families to Lisbon for the boat trip to England. Jaap traveled with false papers, posing as an Austrian teacher traveling in German trains. He now spoke German with an Austrian accent he picked up on holidays before the war. One day, he was taken off the train in Brussels and interrogated for six hours, and then they let him go. On route home, he realized that he had left his suitcase on the platform. When he came home, he rang the doorbell and I opened the door. He ran past me to the stairs and ran up to his room. I heard the bedroom door slam shut and then I heard crying for a long time.

This war caused many changes in people's lives and plans, even well made ones; they often had to be changed because of it. My father's brother Willem was a case in point. At school, he was not a good student. At his elementary school teachers coming to his home gave him extra lessons and sometimes he went to the home of a teacher in a nearby town. He was like a wild bird in a cage, and would rather be outside than in class. In secondary school he did not do well either and never graduated. When war was declared in 1914, he was called up for military service and his father and his brother Arnold brought him to the train, heavily packed and in uniform. It was on that day that Arnold declared that he was engaged to Isabella van Styrum. When Willem came out of the army, he tried to get work, but without diplomas, it was almost impossible. Arnold discussed this problem with his brother-in-law, Carel Begeer and Willem was hired to work in the factory. The job was not a full-time one and he was bored. He took a job in Germany, where the owner of a large factory in Hamburg offered him work.

The owner and his wife were millionaires, but they did not have any children. They liked Willem and offered him a place to stay with them. He became the son they never had. Willem had a dog, and it followed him through the factory. One day, Willem wanted to take the elevator down. He opened the door, but since it was dark, he could not see that the elevator was not at the floor. He fell down the lift house and was now lying at the bottom, when all of a sudden the elevator came down towards him.

The dog started to bark and the elevator was stopped just in the nick of time. Willem was brought to the hospital, where he was operated on to remove a bone chip from his knee. The company paid the costs and Willem returned to Holland, where he started as a clerk at a flourmill. The mill burned down and Willem was without a job again.

His father Willem and Umma Co decided that he would be better off in a country like America and in 1923 he left for the new world. Meanwhile he had married Allegonda Klarenbeek and when the young couple left, they took with them a two-year old daughter, Ingeborg Flora. After arriving in New York, Willem went immediately to the Dutch consulate. He knew the son of the consul and thought that it might be a good introduction. The consul advised him to go to Detroit, where he might get a job at one of the automobile plants. He took the advice and the young family arrived in Detroit, where he went to the Ford plant. He did not get a job there, but he remembered seeing a Head Office building of General Motors. There he asked to see the President and after talking to him for two hours, he was given two letters of introduction, one for the President of Chevrolet and the other for the President of Cadillac.

When he met the President of Chevrolet, he took out of his pocket a medal, struck at Begeer, where he had a job for a while. He was offered a job as a drill press operator. From this beginning, he became a Public Relations manager for a large Insurance company, The Auto Owners, while his wife Gonda, produced two more daughters. He was appointed Dutch honorary Consul for Detroit and he organized a state visit of Queen Juliana in 1952, for which he was decorated. They recognized his many talents. He was a true pioneer.

His three daughters were named Flora, Helen and Gertrude and when they graduated from high school, they were given a choice of a gift. Either an automobile, or a visit to Holland and Flora chose the latter. In 1939, Flora arrived in Holland, but the timing was not on her side. In the fall, it was decided that she should return home in a hurry. Already it was known that only a few flights would leave for the United States and Flora went to the American consulate in The Hague. There she stood in line with many other Americans wanting to go home. Ahead of her was another American and she had a long conversation with him while they waited. He was obviously attracted to this blond girl and then he said: "How would you like to go back to the States, and have your ticket paid for to boot?" "Sure" she answered. That looked good, she thought. "I am the personal secretary of Mrs. Rath, from New York. She is an old lady and she can use a companion to help her on the trip", he said. When the German troops entered the country on May 10, 1940, Flora immediately tried to get a seat on a plane. It was not until May 1941 that she was able to find a way home. Mrs. Rath was her ticket out of the country, her ticket home, but she was not able to go directly. Strange as it may sound, but she had to take a train to Berlin. Mrs. Rath was not the only person, apart from Flora, in her party. The director of the travel agency wanted to get out as well. When they arrived in Berlin, they checked into Hotel Berlin. The next day they flew from Tempelhof Airport to Estoril in Portugal. On arrival the plane made an emergency landing at the airport in Madrid, because the runways were flooded after a torrential rain. "Leave me here" Mrs. Rath told Flora "You go along and I'll see you when we leave. I have my typewriter here and I will amuse myself". Flora was carried on the shoulders of the crewmembers to the terminal.

I don't know if they eventually fetched old Mrs. Rath, but we knew that the male crewmembers enjoyed the company of this girl and organized a party on the spot. After six hours they left for New York where Flora parted from Mrs. Rath. She had given her a ticket back home to Detroit. The American Branch of the family was complete again. My father asked Flora before she left, if she could contact Princess Juliana, who had left for Canada with her daughters Beatrix and Irene. One day a letter arrived from the Red Cross, containing a photograph of Flora, flanked by Princess Juliana and the Governor General of Canada, the Duke of Athlone. Flora wrote that she spent the day with the Princess telling her about her experiences in occupied Holland. While in Ottawa the Princess gave birth to another daughter, Margriet. The Canadian government declared the floor where she was born Dutch territory as if the new princess had been born in Holland. Her name, Dutch for 'daisy', gave the Dutch the Flower of Hope, although they learned about it in their cellars listening to Radio London in a blacked out home.

Chapter Three
_____

Tax Collector

My grandparents lived near the palace/town hall in Wassenaar, in fact they lived so close by, that the stables were across the street. They were very large, because Prince Frederick used these not only to keep horses and store the carriage, but they also housed his personnel. When the old town hall, near the old church in the centre of town became too small, the town bought the palace, with all the grounds and the stables in 1929 and they moved into its new quarters. At that time, some elderly people who were in the service of the prince while he was alive still lived there. The town used the stables partly to house the fire department trucks and as a garage for other vehicles. Woods surrounded the backyard of my grandparent's house and in the fall, apple trees were full of fruit. Rudolf and I loved to play there. Sometimes, after a rain, the backyard had patches of mud and we sought out these patches in particular to live out our fantasies. On our return, our mother was not too pleased, because we had mud all over us. Then, a week later, we would say to each other, "Let's go to Umma Co and play in the mud again". Grandfather Willem, had retired from the Department of Internal Revenue, where he was inspector, with many people under him. He had made quite a career for himself, a career that started at the beginning of the First World War. His father-in-law was also an inspector and no doubt he used his influence to get his son-in-law in the department. He had studied tax law and was well prepared for his chosen profession. We called our grandmother Umma Co. Umma Co was a talented woman. She was an artist, although she would not give herself that title. For her it was just a hobby, but when looking at the many samples of her work, one has to conclude that she was gifted.

Umma Co was descended from an old Dutch family, Krayenhoff, whose illustrious member, General C. R. T Krayenhoff was a famous topographer, who made a map of the different scales and field surveys and through triangulation was able to use church towers to make an accurate map. It took him from 1802-1811 to complete his work. After the annexation of the Kingdom of Holland by the French Empire, the sheets and copper plates were transported to Paris where the work continued for another four years. Krayenhoff was also a military engineer and was Inspector General of all the country's fortifications. Just after Napoleon captured Holland, he was Minister of Defense. He met Napoleon and tried to reason with him. Napoleon's brother eventually came to Holland to take over the region. His brother wanted to pull cannons all over the countryside until the general took his walking stick and pushed it into the ground. The water table was so high that his cane went into the ground like butter. When my grandparents were elderly, they moved into a senior citizen's home.

One day, my father came home with a tray full of ladies' watches. He had picked up a tray from the big Begeer store in The Hague, one of the many stores in Holland and other countries operated by the company he worked for. Rudolf and I had planned to give Umma Co a watch for her birthday and we thought that she should have the choice. When we arrived at the door, we heard our grandfather yelling at Umma Co: "Don't yell so much, I'm not deaf". But he was getting deaf and refused a hearing aid. He was a proud man. Umma Co looked at the watches on the tray and she chose the smallest one. "These children should not spend so much money on me", she thought. "Don't you think that a bigger face would be better?" we offered. "I'm not blind" she answered. She was proud too. She never realized that the smallest watch was the most expensive one on the tray.

Opa, that was what we called our grandfather, used to tell us stories from the time he was a boy. When my father heard about the stories, he was mad. Perhaps he was afraid that we would get into trouble by trying to try the same shenanigans. But Opa's stories were those from another time, when horses and carriages were the order of the day. He never told us about his adventures as a tax collector; we learned of those later.

When he had a post at the border, some of these adventures could be quite dangerous. Smugglers abounded in those days. At one time Opa administered a large region containing two cities and five towns. In one of the cities, a large distillery tried hard to reduce their taxes, by smuggling and other crafty means. My grandfather was too smart for them. Each barrel had a number, corresponding with the numbers on the manifests. They had to pay taxes on each barrel produced. They bought barrels with identical numbers. That seemed a bright idea, but one day, one of these barrels sprang a small leak and they had to cover the hole with a copper plate.

Each barrel contained 273 liters of 50 proof brandy. To make their little scheme work, they had to place an identical plate on the duplicate barrel. The inspector and his men were looking outside from a ditch and watched the barrels rolled out to be shipped outside the town line. The inspector really inspected well, because, thanks to binoculars, he discovered one barrel with 28 nails through the copper plate and the other had 37 nails. He levied heavy fines, 25,000 guilders for loss of revenue and an additional 75,000 for the fraud. The distillery was now afraid about the publicity that would come and they tried to have the fines reduced. Opa did not like bribery and as a result, after trying, they were able to decrease the fine to 85,000 guilders.

At the end of his career Opa was offered the position of President of a large textile concern and another one to manage the French railway office in The Hague, but he declined both jobs. In the middle of the war, my grandparents were evacuated to a town in the middle of the country. I suspect that the Germans did not want any residents near the V2 launching site in front of the town hall. In the summer of 1944, they returned to Wassenaar and moved in with a widow across the street from where we lived. My grandfather always told us that he wanted to live to see the end of this terrible war. He outlived the war by nine months. He had two passions in life, his work and his children. It is strange, that in the stories he wrote in, one person was never mentioned, and that was Umma Co. He lived through two wars and into modern times. He tried to adjust to an environment that changed very rapidly.

Chapter Four

_____

Yet Another Painter In The Family

The 7th child of Opa's grand parents was Dorothea (Thee) Arnoldine von Weiler, born in Arnhem, 17th December 1866 and she died in Amsterdam February 14, 1956. She lived the most part of her life with her mother for whom she cared for until her mother's death in 1907. Thee was bossy, and the relationship between these two women was not always pleasant. She did the housework, because she maintained that her mother was not capable enough, something her mother disputed all the time. After her mother died, she married a wine merchant Marius Albert van Andriga de Kempenaar. Marius however died suddenly after five months of marriage.

She found solace in her painting. She studied with a very well known artist at the time, Theophile de Bock and was a student of Hendrick Willebord Jansen (1855-1908). She had a number of exhibitions. She was a sister of my grandfather Willem Carel von Weiler. She followed her grandfather in his footsteps and he was another well known painter in our family Coenraad Alexander Weerts. Here are some details:

Arnold Carl von Weiler (February 3, 1819-December 26, 1891) married Zwanida Johanna Dorothea Emilia Weerts (October 30, 1823- June 30, 1907). She was the daughter of Coenraad Alexander Weerts and Anna Maria de Jongh. Coenraad was the painter C.A.Weerts. Their oldest son was Willem Carel von Weiler (October 14, 1860- February 24, 1946). Dorothea was the painter of the painting in the possession of Glenn von Weiler. Willem Carel had two daughters and a son. The son was Arnold Carl, who was born June 6,1892 and died 101 years and six months later. He was my father.

FIVE DAYS OF WAR

Day One: Friday May 10, 1940

Winston Churchill left No. 10 Downing Street and was thinking how ironic it was, that on the very day he was called to power, he had a full-blown war on his hands. For eight years, he had warned Parliament of the onslaught of Adolf Hitler and his gang, but it had been all in vain, now the news from the continent was troubling. Earlier, at 4.30 in the morning, the German offence had begun. As many as 42 transport planes, each hauling a team of airborne troops flew over Belgium and the gliders sailed silently over the flatlands. At the same time a large contingent of tanks and troops broke over the borders of Belgium, Luxembourg and Holland, two million soldiers with powerful weapons. The first wave consisted of 4,000 troops, paratroopers, infantry and cavalry divisions headed for highways and bridges. The Dutch had hoped to cut off the troops before the Germans could destroy the vital bridges, but they were already too late. While the defenders were still trying to assemble the troops, the Germans captured the bridges after which the tanks and other heavy weapons came in from the border. The Dutch were not prepared for such an attack. After the initial assault, infantry and artillery were able to drive the Germans from three airfields surrounding The Hague by evening. This saved the capital and the government for the moment.

The Germans were planning to capture the Queen and the government, but this plan failed and it took many days before the attackers could fulfill their plans at least partially. Near The Hague, bombs fell at 4 o'clock on the new military barracks. Some soldiers left in pajamas, while a number of bombs fell through the roofs. Sixty men were killed immediately, while another hundred or so were wounded, when they fell through the floor on top of the horses, which were in panic. The day before, the ministers were called in for an emergency meeting, which broke up at two o'clock in the morning for a short rest. Defense minister Dyxhoorn left for his department office where he had a cot. His two assistants already stayed overnight in their offices for the last three days. At 2.30 in the morning he had a short chat with them, and then he retired. The moment he laid down, in his clothes, he heard airplanes overhead. At three o'clock he was called by one of his assistants. Messages had come in about the bombardment of Rotterdam Harbour. The minister immediately contacted the Prime Minister and it was decided to send coded messages to London, Brussels and Paris. After receipt, the ambassadors were ordered to open a secret envelope with instructions and a message from the supreme commander of the Allied Forces.

Now the Prime Minister and the Defense minister called the ministers again for a second emergency meeting, now at the home of one of the ministers. The meeting was at 5.30 in the morning. The Defense minister left in a hurry to the meeting, under artillery fire and the noise of airplanes flying over. The Prime Minister had to leave early, because he expected a visit from the German ambassador, who had given notice, that he had an important message to give. The other ministers started to write a message for the citizens of the country. They also discussed the very serious situation. Then they decided to break up and to meet again at the Economic affairs building, which had a bomb shelter.

The Prime Minister left for his office to meet the ambassador, when a young soldier stopped him. He told him to let him through, that he was the Prime Minister, but he had his orders and was not to let him through. Meanwhile German planes flew low over the palace, and were shooting at them. It took a number of telephone calls and about twenty minutes, before he stepped into his office. Only minutes later two officers brought in the ambassador. He had a short note in his hands from Adolf Hitler, which demanded unconditional surrender. But he could not talk, because he was crying and his tears streamed down his cheeks. He could not read the note either, and the minister said to him just to hand over the note.

He wrote a short answer and gave it to the ambassador, who was then led away by the two officers, still crying, clenching the note in his shaking hand. His wonderful life had collapsed. He had lived in Wassenaar for a number of years, the place he loved, close to the beach and the dunes in a park like setting, with large stately homes, built by the captains of industry in Rotterdam, owners of shipping lines and other large corporations, but these mansion like homes were now occupied by the ambassadors of many countries, outside the city, which housed the government of the country.

Day Two: Saturday, May 11, 1940

The German offense continued unabated and with speed. The Dutch army realized it was no match for this massive attack. Increasingly, the Germans were capturing more territory, but they were surprised that this was not the easy walk they expected. When the Dutch flooded parts of the country, the Germans dropped airborne troops behind the water, and increasingly it became evident, that it was impossible to withstand this enemy. In the midst of this chaos, Carl von Weiler made preparations to be sent to England. He was an electrical engineer, a professor of engineering at the Technical University of Delft, a reserve naval officer and an inventor. He was the director of the Laboratory of electronic development for the armed forces in The Hague and in that capacity, he had developed sophisticated electronic instruments for the Artillery, the Navy and other branches of the armed forces.

One of his accomplishments was the development of Radar, which was simultaneously being developed in England by Watson-Watt and in France. After his first wife, Eugenie died in 1939 he had a young son, Paul, who was four, when the war broke out. Carl remarried Olga Blaauw also in 1939 and a week before the Germans attacked the country, his second son Gerard was born. Paul moved in with his maternal grandparents after his mother died. Carl expected to be picked up any day and realized that his family had to stay behind. He gathered up two suitcases, one for his clothes and another for his drawings and other important and secret papers and waited at home. It was not until Tuesday however, that he was picked up, because authorities had their hands full arranging for the departure of the Royal Family.

Queen Wilhelmina was urged on Thursday, to move out of her palace at the outskirts of the city into a bunker on the grounds. She was in contact with armed forces at all times. A few hours after the attack on the barracks, an attaché had told her that a German plane was shot down, not far from the palace. When more paratroopers landed her private secretary urged her to move her with her family into the city, where protection was easier to accomplish. The Royal Family left for the palace in the city where they moved into a small bunker on the grounds. The queen was disappointed, that she was not allowed to visit the wounded in the hospitals and only half believed stories about fighting in the streets. Even the ministers were in bunkers at the time, where all the preparations were made to eventually bring the queen and her family to England.

Princess Juliana and her husband Bernhard, tried to leave on Friday the tenth, but that was impossible, because Germans were everywhere and the plan had to be postponed. But on Sunday the situation seemed somewhat better and it was decided to bring the Royal Family with armoured cars from the National Bank to the naval port of Ijmuiden, where they boarded an English destroyer. Later Prince Bernhard, who was head of the armed forces, would leave again to return to Belgium.

Day Four: Monday May 13, 1940

Early in the morning, the queen left with her family. At the same time enemy tanks reached Rotterdam and the enemy was getting close. The queen packed a small suitcase and the armoured cars departed at 9.30 with police escort to the naval port. The members of her government would follow later. Meanwhile in Rotterdam, the Germans had trouble breaking through bridgeheads. Hitler then lost his patience and decided to bomb the city into submission. In the car with the queen was a general and another officer, both armed with pistols. The Dutch navy had left earlier for England, as it was needed for the Allied Forces. This was a very difficult time for the queen, who wanted to be with her people in this crisis. But it had to be done. The government would govern from London for the time being.

The queen arrived at Buckingham Palace, where she would be a guest and immediately after her arrival, she issued a proclamation to the Dutch people. She mentioned that this was a very difficult situation, but she would do her utmost to look after the interest of her people. That she was doing in spades, and during the war she was nicknamed "The difficult Old Lady" in parliamentary circles.

Day Five: Tuesday May 14, 1940

It was 2 o'clock and the streets were deserted. The black, unmarked car had stopped in front of Carl's house and the naval officer rang the doorbell. It awoke the family, but Carl was already dressed. He picked up his two suitcases, already waiting in the hall, kissed his wife Olga and his little baby son, and left the house. Would he ever see his family again? He knew that his services were now needed in England, but he was not anxious to go into a submarine under the circumstances. The car made one more stop to pick up his colleague Max Staal. They both were heavily involved at the laboratory and now their only concern was to safeguard their drawings and notes. Now the car was speeding through the silence of the night. The driver, a naval officer, did not talk much and when they arrived at a small fishing harbour, the submarine was waiting for them. They boarded the vessel quickly and the submarine left immediately, going down as soon as they reached open water. They were undetected and arrived in England by daybreak.

The drawings they had with them were in particular of the new listening device for the detection of airplanes, later named Radar, which is an acronym for Radio Detection and Ranging Device. Early in 1939, a prototype of this Radar device was ready and Carl wanted to give a demonstration to Prince Benhard, but it was a very foggy day and initially the demonstration was a fiasco, until he directed the device towards the church steeples at the horizon, and now he could detect Roman Catholic churches due to the iron crosses on the steeples. Two prototypes were ready on the day the Germans attacked the country,. One was installed at an artillery installation near the city and the other was installed on the last day of the five day war and brought to England by the Royal Navy.

Other material in the laboratory was destroyed. Carl von Weiler and Max Staal were immediately appointed to the Admiralty Signal Establishment and assigned to develop a 50cm radar device, which was eventually installed in the Dutch destroyer H.M. Isaac Sweers, which had left earlier for England. This Radar device gave excellent service guiding the cannons aboard ship in the Mediterranean.

When I grew up, I did not really know Paul and Gerard. As it turned out, the family members did not associated with them, because they were Roman Catholic, like their mother. My father Arnold was very annoyed about this situation, and decided to do something about it. He invited Paul and Gerard for dinner and invited as many family members as he could find. As it turned out we all were very enthusiastic about our newfound cousins, and they became such close friends, that when Paul was married and his wife was getting a son, this boy was named after my father. He was thrilled.

In 1942 a German destroyer sank a Dutch one, near the coast of Africa. During the entire war, Carl was intimately involved in the development of Radar. He was also a consultant to American Radar developers. Carl is known in the Netherlands as the father of Radar. He certainly did his bid for the war effort.

The Germans had considerable problems on this Tuesday. The tanks could not get across the Rotterdam bridges, since the Dutch had sealed the ends. The strong German airborne forces had either been captured or dispersed. During the morning, Hitler issued a directive stating that the power of resistance of the Dutch had proved to be much stronger than anticipated. He then ordered the bombing of Rotterdam. This happened on the same day and the heart of Holland's second largest city was wiped out. The surrender of the city then was sealed.

Day Six, Wednesday, May 15, 1940

At eleven o'clock in the morning, the Dutch army capitulated. The five-day war was over. The air force was destroyed, although some airplanes were able to fly to England, the artillery was now silent and now the country's citizens would live trapped by the Germans for the coming five years. The spirit of the Dutch people was not broken however, which was shown during the dark days ahead.

When the war started, I was fourteen years old and I was not really aware what was happening around me. I saw German soldiers everywhere and heard that a number of mansions in the Kieviet section of the town had been confiscated, but I normally went to school and my father went to Voorschoten, a nearby town, where he worked in the silver factory for his Brother-in-law Carel Begeer. In the factory everyone was furiously at work to safeguard the valuable items made out of silver and gold and the boxes with precious stones waiting to be set into jewelry. In front of the factory, large flowerbeds were dug up and men were digging big holes. Then large wooden crates full of finished products and boxes with very valuable contents were buried in the holes. Then the flowerbeds were filled with soil and now gardeners again planted flowers and bushes if nothing had happened.

The company had large stores in big cities in Holland, and even in the Netherlands Indies and after the bombing of Rotterdam, they heard that the store there was hit; in fact, all the stores in the plaza were destroyed. There was great concern about the valuable merchandise and they hoped that they were safely stored in the walk-in safe. It was impossible to go to Rotterdam, however and they just had to wait until things cooled down. I myself went with my bike to the outskirts of The Hague, planning to have a look in Rotterdam, but I had to turn back, as even outside The Hague the heat was too great. Eventually they went to have a look and the safe seemed fine, but after a closer look they found that the heat had warped the door and they had a big problem on their hands. When they did open the door eventually, they found only one mountain of metal on the floor over a meter high, it was a mountain of silver, gold and platinum, imbedded with precious stones. Oddly enough some silver forks and spoons were sticking out in a number of places. I often wondered how they were able to get it out of the safe.

Before the war, when I was nine, my father took me to a concert in the Hague to hear the famed Residentie orchestra. I had never been at a concert before, and since I was learning to play the violin, I was anxious to go with him. When we arrived at the concert hall we were caught in a line up, since my father did not have any tickets. When it was our turn, we learned that they had only one ticket left and my father explained that he wanted one for his son as well. The cashier then talked to a uniformed man and he took me through a long corridor at the end of which we entered a door on the left. When he opened the door the room I saw behind the door a room fully lit and when we entered I saw that I was now behind the orchestra. The man brought a chair and placed it not far from the kettledrums. All the chairs were empty and one bass was leaning against a chair. I looked across the rows of chairs to see into the hall if I saw my dad, but I didn't. Then the musicians came in carrying their instruments, the musicians started to play their instruments, but that was not music, just noise. Then a man with a violin played one note and walked from chair to chair to give the musicians a chance to tune their instruments.

Then everybody sat down and then the conductor came into the room holding his little stick. He turned to the audience and bowed, then he turned to us and gave the sign that they should start to play. The man with the large drum started to bang on them even before the musicians started to play. I saw an instrument I had never seen, and it looked like a long pipe and at the end a little one in the man's mouth. I wanted to see better and I slid my chair towards him, and every time I saw something interesting I moved my chair a bit further to see better, not realizing that now I sat in the orchestra. When the music stopped, the conductor turned around and bowed again and at the end of the concert he did that again and turned to the orchestra and lifted his hands to make the musicians stand up, and when they did, I stood up too. I realized that I should not have done that and I sat down again and I wondered if the conductor had seen me doing that. While I stood up for a second I saw my father sitting there and I wondered if he had seen me sitting in the orchestra. This was a concert I never forget, it made me realize how wonderful music can be in my life and now I was anxious to learn to play as well as the people I met sitting in the orchestra.

CHAPTER SIX

WASSENAAR

The highway from Amsterdam to The Hague runs past the lush green fields of farms and past the City of Leiden, but the moment it reaches Wassenaar, it runs through the outskirts of town. A bit further a large acreage of lush grass fields and in the background the town hall, which used to be a Royal palace. In front, large trees on either side of the palace and a fountain in front of the building, a marble one in the form of a bathtub flanked on either side by marble lions spouting water. Czar Alexander donated this fountain to the Royal residents, giving the town a beautiful setting for spring weddings. Behind the town hall a large pond with ducks and swans with a large forested area as a backdrop.

The town itself is behind this beautiful setting. Behind the forest area you'll find the Prinsenweg, or Prince Road, the street I lived in a good part of my youth. This road is very wide, because the yellow two-wagon streetcar from The Hague to Leiden, ran through the middle. Now the streetcar has disappeared but the two-way roads remain. Large homes occupy either side, duplexes on our side and single homes on the other. The owner of our home, who lived in Amsterdam, never wanted to sell that home to my parents although they tried hard enough. There were a number of soccer fields, an inside swimming pool and a senior citizens complex, with balconies overlooking the soccer fields at the end of the road, giving seniors good seats to view the activities below. My parents eventually lived there.

Across the fields and a connecting road there were two mansions with blue glazed clay tile roofs. Two brothers of the Ruys family who were wealthy shipping magnates, owned these homes. Further on, towards The Hague was a large section of the town filled with more mansions in a wooded area, with swimming pools and the owners, all captains of industry chose this area to build their mansions because of the close proximity to The Hague, the Government and the embassies. Later, most mansions were sold to other countries to be used as residences of their ambassadors. Now they have wrought iron fences and security cameras but still, town folk just, like before the war, find employment as gardeners, maids, domestics and nannies for the children.

Behind the Prinsenweg are a number of streets with homes, some shops and the Langstraat, in the centre of town. It used to be open for cars, but now only delivery trucks are admitted and it is now strictly for shopping afoot or on bike. At the end the old town square with, in the middle, a large old-fashioned pump. The square surrounded by buildings from another century and at one side an 11th century church surrounded by a wrought iron fence and a cemetery with old trees. The church is still in use and is beautifully restored to its former glory.

My grandfather was worried that he would not see the end of the Second World War, but he made it, as a half year after the end he died and was buried there. In the years he lived in Wassenaar, walking distance from the town hall, he was very much involved in the community. He was a member of city council and was involved with the Rescue brigade at the beach he loved so much. I visited the church for special reasons. I had a friend, who was organist there an since I took violin lessons, I played with him up in the loft of the organ. I had a number of other friends playing various instruments and we formed a small orchestra and played in the church, which had and still has, wonderful acoustics.

My parents felt that we must learn a musical instrument and since my two brothers and my sister chose the piano, I wanted to play one that was different and I chose the violin. My father played that instrument as well, and he often played alto violin when he played with his friends. The teachers gave lessons at home and I had to study before breakfast and going to school, while my father was shaving upstairs. If I did something wrong, he either stamped his foot on the floor or yelled at me to do it over again.

Next door lived the family Weynman with two children in their early twenties and their mother was an accomplished musician and singer and we made music together, she on her grand piano and I on my violin. Now when I hear music on the radio, and hear a piece that I used to play with her, I am surprised. I must be a much better player than I remembered.

Behind the church runs a road we took to the beach. We first pass hockey fields where I played hockey, when I was a youth and then the road goes through the dunes, past a hotel ending in a parking area. From there we walked to the sandy beach and looking out on the North sea, you could see beach restaurants and wicker beach chairs for rent and shower cabins for the swimmers and the beach reaches very far on either side. Near the dunes, a road to other beach towns and further past bulb fields every spring ablaze with red and white and yellow colours. Wassenaar is certainly a prosperous town. Now the Crown Prince and princess, born in Argentine are living there.

On the other side of the highway to The Hague or Amsterdam is the road to the town where the silver factory was and where my father had his office. Carel Begeer was a very talented designer of silver articles and his drawings are now in a museum. My father's passion was medals and decorations. He produced commemorative medals and he had a large list of artists, sculptors and poets to choose from. Often if someone's portrait was to be on a medal, he contacted one of his artists, and then a poet to write a suitable inscription or line around the portrait. When my parents had an important anniversary, he contacted a sculptor he liked and had a double portrait made and then it was produced in the factory. One day he gave all of us a medal just for that occasion. We marveled at the likeness and then I saw on the back a little apple tree wedged in a corner. I asked my father why that apple tree had four apples on the tree and one on the ground, and then, reluctantly, he explained that between my self and my seven-year, older brother was one other child that lived only a few days and had not been named yet. Now I knew why my younger brother Rudolf and I grew up together, while my older brother Jaap and my sister Flory, who was nine years older than I, were already out of the house and at university in Leiden to study law and at University hospital to study nursing. That subject never was talked about and now I had found out accidentally.

28

CHAPTER SEVEN

FIVE YEARS OF WAR

Everyday, we took our bikes to school, and there they tried hard not to change the regular school program, but sometimes that was very difficult. At home, our parents wanted to keep our family dinners at the same time; my father went to work every morning and my mother stayed home. Before the war they had a live in maid, but when the war started that was soon dispensed with. It was something they grew up with, but now realized that we were living in a different time, where every body had to pitch in and help out as much as we could.

Since Rudolf and I were the only kids in the house, we were aware that Jaap and Flory had a different life. Jaap was a law student and Flory was to be a nurse, but what we did not know was that Jaap during his student years was involved in dangerous work. During that time he was a member of an underground cell in the student community, bringing Jewish families to Paris, where Students at Sorbonne University, took over to bring these people to Lisbon, Portugal where they were smuggled onto fishing boats to sail to London. The dangers involved were obvious. He took international trains and pretended to be an Austrian teacher, which meant, that not only knowledge of the German language was essential, but he also needed to speak with an Austrian accent. Only one holiday in Austria before the war was all he needed to pick up this dialect. He was very musical and had a good ear. When he graduated from high school, part of his exams were oral and he was asked in English what English literature he had read, and he answered: "all plays of Shakespeare".

The examiners were very skeptical and asked to recite something from one of the plays. Now he had his chance to really do his thing, and he started to speak in such a surprising and heavy Scottish accent, that he received a high mark immediately. He was in Scotland one summer and took in a Shakespeare festival.

That he was never caught in the trains was also surprising, because it was obvious that the Germans were on the trains all the time as well. One day, on the way back from Paris, he was taken out of the train in Brussels, taken away into a room at the railway station and interrogated for some six hours during which he never veered away from talking Austrian. Eventually, they let him go, and he boarded another train, but twenty minutes on the way, he remembered that he had left his little suitcase behind on the platform, because he was so very anxious to get out of there. When he arrived home, he rang the bell for some reason, and I happened to open the door. He ran past me, up the stairs to his old room, slammed the door, and I heard him crying for a long time. This experience was more than he could endure and his nerves were obviously shot. After the war he was going to receive a decoration, but he never went to the Hague to pick it up. We can only guess why; he did not wanted to get into the limelight, in fact, he never talked to anyone about his experiences, and what we know, we heard from third parties. A couple of female students were involved in the same cell, but they were able to escape the train, realizing that the train was being raided by soldiers.

While working in a hospital, it was not unusual, that Flory would meet a young doctor. Jo Bok came from a doctor's family as his father was a brainsurgeon and other members were either doctors or in any other way were associated with the medical profession. He was destined to great things, as he would eventually direct a civic hospital in Dordrecht, near Rotterdam. But first there was to be a wedding, in his case it had to be under the eyes of the Germans, who could use a talented doctor. The wedding was to be held from our home in Wassenaar, a walking distance from the town hall. Flory and Jo walked over to the ambulance department of the hospital where they were ready for the young couple. Flory was dressed in nurse's uniform and Jo had a white coat on, a blood pressure cup around his neck and they boarded the ambulance.

It was Saturday, February 11, 1943 and the idea was to drive to

Wassenaar, in an ambulance, to prevent the Germans from stopping them, go home, change, get married and return to Rotterdam and back to work. The weather was mild and it was sunny. The ambulance sped over the highway and stopped in front of the house. There everything had been arranged there as well. They went upstairs to my parent's bedroom and changed. Meanwhile, other family members and friends arrived and when everybody was ready, we all walked out of the driveway to the end of the road, crossed the road near the sports fields, into the pathway and into the forest. Halfway, we had to cross a wide footbridge and I was at the head of the parade. Being the first on the footbridge, I turned around and said, "Stop". "Your faces are looking too serious. You are not allowed to cross this bridge until you have a smile on your face". This caused an expected reaction and we walked past the pond with the ducks and the swans, around the building to the front and then we passed the fountain with the lions on either side, then we turned left to climb the many steps of our town hall. A uniformed person came down the steps to welcome us. "Welcome to our town hall", he said, "As you enter, if you are not familiar, the wedding room is the first one on the right, but I have one request. Would you please not look at the wall on your left hand side?" Of course, when we entered, that was exactly what we all did. We saw portraits of Adolf Hitler and the local German commander, who had taken over the administration of the whole area. After a Town hall official conducted the wedding, we walked back over the footbridge and home to have lunch. The bride and groom changed into their uniforms again and left in the ambulance and in a hurry for the hospital in Rotterdam.

While studying to be a nurse, Flory decided to take courses in tailoring and dressmaking. This was strictly to be a hobby, but during the war years, this became a very useful talent to have, because in wartime clothing became a scarce commodity. My grandparents lived close by, near the stables of the former palace, which were now used for vehicles belonging to the town. They lived in a duplex with a thatched roof. When Rudolf and I grew up in Wassenaar and still small, we walked to our grand parents often. The backyard was sometimes muddy after a rain, and Rudolf and I loved playing in the mud and my mother was dismayed that Umma Co let us do that. We called our grandmother Umma Co and she always said to my mother:" Let them have their fun". When the war broke out, German soldiers surrounded Umma Co and Opa. Living so close to the town hall was not always pleasant, because the Germans had decided, that in front of the town hall; on the grassy field was a good spot to establish a launching pad for giant V2 rockets.

Early one morning, a long mobile rocket launcher came in from the highway, and parked in front of the marble fountain. A large truck behind with men dressed in asbestos uniforms were ordered out of the truck and now they were standing in line waiting for instructions. The officer explained what they would have to do. These men were taken out of a German prison camp, and they were going to be the rocket launchers. The officer explained that if they would escape, they would be shot. These men were dispensable, while soldiers were needed at the front. It was dangerous work and the officer knew that at first 80% of all launchings were failure bound. The first one was launched, but while high in the sky, the engines failed and the big rocket crashed down to earth. The prisoners were not hurt, because the rocket came down in a farmer's field and exploded. All of the windows in front of the town hall were broken except some round glass windows; they were still in tact.

Our parents, Rudolf and I were sitting at the dinner table for supper and I was facing the front window when, all of a sudden, I saw a big silvery object appear from the back of the houses on the other side of the street, then I saw fire and I did not hear anything, and I yelled for the others to look. I did not have any idea what that was and when my father saw it too, he told us to duck under the table. Then we heard engines roaring for a minute and then silence. Then the sound of an enormous explosion and all front windows were shattered. It was odd that the windows at the rear of the house were still in tact, and, looking out through the window hole, the windows of the homes across the road were intact as well. As it turned out, their back windows were all shattered. My father grabbed a rug, a hammer and nails and nailed the rug over the window, since the window frame was made of steel, he had to tack the rug against the wall. From that day on, many rockets were launched, because London was just opposite Wassenaar across the North Sea. The failure rate dropped over time and many bombs fell on the city of London.

In our town lived a KLM pilot, who at the beginning of the war had fled to join the Royal Air force in England. He was eventually assigned to knock out the launching place in Wassenaar, because he knew every nook and cranny of our town. In the middle of the night flying over in the dark and all alone, he bombed the site with precision and later, when we walked over to get a look, we saw dead horses hanging in the trees and bomb craters around the launching site. Dead prisoners in asbestos suits were scattered around. They never knew what hit them. We were wondering about the dead horses. As it turned out, due to lack of fuel, they had confiscated horses in town to haul the launchers. When the war was over, the pilot came home, and when he entered his home, there was nobody there to greet him. Later he was told that his wife had left for Germany with a soldier. He never saw her again.

One day, the principal came into our class. He told us that the German soldiers were now getting into the schools to look for able-bodied teenagers to work in the munitions factories in Germany. So many men were in the armed forces, that they were looking elsewhere for workers. He warned us to be careful and when the bell sounded, only once, it meant that some of the bigger kids had to hide. Another problem was with Jewish kids. In a number of classes were students of the Jewish faith, and they also had to hide. Before the war, the school was enlarged and a second story and an attic were added. Every class, with Jewish kids had one student being responsible to get these kids up into the attic. Our class had a set of twin girls, and I was selected to get them upstairs. Instead of stairs, they cleaned out a large cupboard in the hall and installed a rope ladder, which could be hauled up. When the bell rang, I ran with the girls to the hall cupboard, climbed the rope ladder, hauled it up and closed the hatch and then we waited until the coast was clear. We did not believe that this would ever happen, but it did. German soldiers entered the school, looked everywhere, but left empty handed.

We had an excellent English language teacher, very strict and very particular, when it comes to grammar. She was a spinster and lived with her older sister, also a spinster, in a home near the school. They were both Jewish and her sister did not dared to come out of the house. Miss Ephraim, was rather courageous, but eventually she did not dare to go out into the street either. We asked the principal about her. Was she sick? Is she coming back? The principal explained why she felt she had to stay at home. We discussed the problem among ourselves and decided that, if she cannot go out of the house, she could not buy groceries. We decided to collect food. Every student would take something from home, and one would bring a basket or a box. We put the basket near the back door. We never saw her again. We don't know what happened to these two women, but we can guess.

One girl in our class was Marion Hartog. She lived in the Kieviet Park and her father was the president of Unilever, the international meat packing company. It was getting dangerous for that Jewish family as well. But they did have an apartment bordering Central Park in New York and Marion expected to move to New York soon, which she and her family did. At the time it was still possible to fly out of Lisbon but getting there was a huge problem. Fortunately, they had the resources and managed to flee the country under the eyes of the Germans. I remember that once I was invited to eat chicken at her home. I was picked up with a limousine and a uniformed chauffeur and when we sat at the dinner table with sterling silver knives, forks and spoons and footmen in uniform and wearing white gloves, were standing behind us to serve.

I learned very fast that I had to keep eating, because if I stopped for a moment, my plate would disappear. Later, in Ontario, I met Marion again. Her father lived in New York now and she had married a boy, who was at our school one class higher. He wanted to start a large pig farm, something I thought odd, as he was Jewish as well. But his father bought a farm for him, gave him a thousand pigs and they then settled in Ontario. A few years later, they divorced and the farm was sold. I never saw either of them since.

My parents were very concerned that Rudolf and I might be picked up by the German patrols. When they were in the street, the telephones were ringing off the hook as all the neigbours warned each other. One day the doorbell rang and because it was summer and quite warm, I had my shorts on. When I opened the door, a German soldier, weapon in hand, stood before me, and immediately he placed his boot inside de door. He had a slip of paper in his hands with my name on it. I don't quite know

34

why I reacted so fast. I told him that it was my older brother and I had not seen him in four months. He seemed satisfied and left. The next time, another soldier actually stepped into the house. He was looking for copper items. The munitions factories in Germany were short of this metal and they would grab any copper they could lay their hands on. The neighbours warned us, and I crawled into my hiding place just in time. We had sliding doors between the living room and the dining room, which had cupboards on either side and, in either room. Over the sliding doors was a space, just for one person, the bottom of which was covered with thin plywood. I had a blanket in there and a chamber pot for emergencies and some light came through on the sides.

Now I heard the German soldiers walking with their boots on the wooden parquet floor below and then I heard a click, which meant that my worst fear would be coming through. The soldier had clicked a bayonet on top his rifle and now he was standing right under me. I held my breath and then, with a strong push, he pushed the pointed bayonet into the thin plywood. I was laying on my side and I saw the bayonet point just clear my legs. I held my hand over my mouth and then saw the bayonet disappear. Meanwhile they saw a small antique wooden box on the table and they tried to open it with the thought that it was a box with a small gun. It was locked and my mother reluctantly turned over the little key. When they opened the box, they saw two fancy curved bottles, each with a silver label hanging on a silver chain with engraved the words BRANDY and WHISKEY. They eagerly grabbed the bottles, removed the tops and started drinking. Then they spitted on the floor in disgust. It turned out to be cold tea, just the colour of the former drinks, not anymore available in the stores.

Still another time, they were picking up radios. People were eagerly listening to Radio London to get the latest news and to get coded messages for the members of the underground. The Germans could not control this and decided to round up as many radios as they could get. Again, they went door to door and people gave them their radios for which they would get a receipt. If they had two radios they gave one and hid the other. When my father had a jubilee, working for Begeer, the company gave him a large radio. The company had produced bronze decorations for the front and my father was given one of the first of the production. Back in the office, my father was asked if he had found a good place to hide his new gift and he told them, that he was worried about his sons, and had given the radio to the Germans. He was simply afraid. "You did what?" they asked him "Did they gave you a receipt? Then his colleague said that he knew the house where they would bring all these radios and he said: "Leave it to me". He went to that house, with a burlap bag under his arms, past the soldier at watch near the front door and saw all kinds of radios all over the floor. This big one, he spotted immediately, draped the burlap over it and walked out, the street out and then he walked to our house and rang the bell. Now my father had his radio and a receipt for whatever that would be worth.

More and more homes and buildings were confiscated to lodge the troops near The Hague and more people had to find other places to live. Our town had a list just for such an occasion and they gave notice to my parents that now two children were out of the house, we should be able to house a small family. My parents did not have any choice and then they came. An old lady, obviously the mother, a middle aged daughter, single and a middle aged son, also single, oh, yes, and then there was a maid, obviously a woman from the country. Immediately we decided that she was the only normal one of the lot. The daughter worked in the city somewhere and sat in a choir and she had to do her scales every morning and my mother was not amused. The son did nothing, but had a paper in his pocket to show the Germans that he had a mental condition. They occupied the spare rooms and the dining room with the sliding doors now closed permanently. They shared the kitchen with my mother and when she was cooking, the old lady came in to look into the pots. The son, Sicco, was whistling all the time and since he had a harelip, the noise was very penetrating. They had a potbellied stove in the dining room and we had one also because the central heating system was long not operational because of lack of fuel.

One morning Jaap came for a visit and while he was drinking his coffee, a terrible noise came out of the dining room. He walked to the hall en entered the dining room and there was mother sitting in a chair, and Elly, her daughter was standing next to the stove. She had a gash on her

36

forehead and a broken teacup was lying on the floor. "What the devil is going on here?" Jaap asked and the mother said, "they are fighting about who's turn it is to light the stove". He apparently had thrown a teacup at her. When they finally left, out of the cupboard came enough food to feed an army, because they wanted to keep it until the need was high. Strange, because at that time, our own cupboards were bare and all we could get were tulip bulbs and sugar beets. They were responsible for the bathroom downstairs and we used the one upstairs. Out of the downstairs one came three or four mats on top of each other. They never threw anything out.

For us, getting fuel for the stove was always a problem. It was almost impossible to keep supplies we needed and one day, I left the house at five o'clock and walked to the highway to find some wood. I had a saw in my hand and further up, I saw a man hiding behind a tree. I had to be careful not to be seen by the Germans, and I hid myself behind another tree. From my vantage point, I saw a perfect tree, small enough to be cut. Then I looked to see who was behind the other tree. To my surprise, it was Rudolf, who had the same idea and left the house before me.

When I graduated, I had a plan to become a journalist. I went to see the editor of the daily paper in Leiden to get some advice. He told me that the paper had now closed down, because the Germans had stopped all truck transports and they did not have any newsprint anymore. The reason was that there was a strike at the railway and that, since the Germans used the railway to a great extent, they retaliated, and now even food transports were not coming into the coastal areas anymore. He suggested that I waited my time by going to the Amsterdam Typographical School, which was famous all over Europe and attracted students from many countries. Now I was going to school again, but now in Amsterdam. I stayed in a boarding house frequented by students of the various colleges and I started my studies. It was not until after the war that I finished my studies, but then my life took a very different turn.

Food became a problem for the West now. The shelves in the stores were getting empty, and we had to find alternate food items to eat. Of course, food could be had at the black market. Food was scarce and we needed stamps to get it and increasingly, these stamps did not have any value, because there was no food to buy even if you had the stamps. Each person received a certain number of them. Only if you had a certain profession which required more food, like a dockworker or, believe it or not, a ballet dancer, did you get extra stamps. An elderly couple in town planned to walk to a farm, ten kilometers out of town. With a handcar, they started walking along side the highway and they left the highway into a road and to a farm, where they bought a burlap bag of potatoes. Now pushing the cart with the heavy load, and with frequent stops to rest, they walked back towards Wassenaar. Halfway along, the man had a heart attack and died. Now the woman, with all her might lifted her husband on the cart. She started to push the cart, which now was an almost impossible task. Close to the border of the town, a German truck with soldiers stopped in front of her, the solders left the truck to see what she had in the cart. They found the bag of potatoes, which they grabbed and then they left laughing loudly. Now the woman did not have anything anymore, no food, and a dead husband and she was standing on the side of the highway, alone.

CHAPTER EIGHT

MANNA FROM HEAVEN

At the end of 1944 and the beginning of 1945, the population of Holland encountered the worst winter of the Second World War. It was a severe winter and due to a strike at the railroad, the Germans stopped all food transports, but when the strike ended after six weeks, they allowed food transports again, but the railroad was in disarray and the result was that in the Western provinces people were literally starving to death. While the South was liberated already, the transport of coal did not start yet. Gas and electricity was cut off and to heat their homes, people were cutting trees and empty houses were demolished to obtain anything that would burn in a woodstove.. Food was rationed, but the stores were empty. People in the cities traveled to the country, in the hope to find a farm, which still had something to eat. They bartered their valuables for food. In the process, 20,000 people starved to death. Bicycles did not have any tires anymore and since gasoline was not available either, the streets, roads and highways did not have any traffic at all.

Whatever people had to eat, only tulip bulbs and sugar beets were left, was cooked on simple, little woodstoves. A little fire in an empty can to heat whatever they could find was also a very dangerous practice. It was said that dogs and cats were eaten and now people did not have any resistance against diseases. There was, however a black-market, but if the Germans discovered this, the perpetrators were shot on sight. The elderly were too weak to walk. People's bodies reacted in different ways to hunger. Some people were getting so thin that you could see their ribs and the bones in their legs, while other bodies were swelling up with excess liquids. In the end, most died a terrible death. In Amsterdam so many people died, that they were not able to bury them, therefore they were temporarily housed in one of the old churches, on the cold stone floor.

Meanwhile, the Royal Air Force in Britain was preparing Lancaster's with the intention of dropping food into the Western coastal areas. On one day, a very severe snowstorm was present over the North Sea. They tried to fly anyway and all the flyers were getting a heavy dose if motion sickness. They could not see anything either and navigation with maps was impossible. At the moment, when they planned to turn home, the sky broke over the sea and a blue sky was now above them. They flew low, from 150 meters down to 10-15 meters and they flew so low because they hoped to avoid being shot with artillery fire from the Germans, but that did not happen. On the 7th of May one bomber loaded with food was shot and crashed into the sea. Two men survived. A cease-fire was in place, but apparently this information had not reached the German artillerymen. The pilots discovered that dropping bags of flour, sugar, chocolate and other food was more difficult than dropping bombs. Some bags were torn open and people were running towards the drop sight to scoop up what they could. Flying so low was dangerous, but the flyers enjoyed their work so much, that they did not mind. These droppings were made from April 29-May 8 1945 and 300 Lancaster's were involved.

The RAF made 3150 flights and 6685 tons of food was dropped. The Americans made 3700 flights and dropped 5343 tons of food. This was not enough to turn around death due to hunger, but then food transports over land started to come in. The Canadian army made 200 trucks available and after the capitulation of Germany on May 8, 1945, food started to arrive by ship in the harbours of Amsterdam and Rotterdam. My brother Rudolf and I watched when the sky was literally filled with airplanes dropping the food. Thousands of parachutes came down and it was amazing to watch. To my mother's horror, Rudolf climbed up on top of the roof and watched this spectacle straddling with one leg on one side and the other at the other side of the roof. With my Brother-in-law, who was a doctor, specializing in the treatment of patients suffering from starvation, we were very aware of what was going on. It was the blackest period of the war. But we survived.

CHAPTER NINE

LIBERATION

At the end of 1944 and the beginning of 1945, the population in Holland encountered the worst winter of the Second World War. It was a severe winter due to a strike at the railroad. The Germans stopped all food transports, but when the strike ended after six weeks, they allowed food transports again, but the railroad was in disarray and the result was that in the Western provinces people were literally starving to death. While the South was liberated already, the transport of coal did not start yet. Gas and electricity was cut off and to heat their homes, people were cutting trees and empty houses were demolished to obtain anything that would burn in a woodstove.

My father looked for ways to make extra money. To buy food at the black market was getting very expensive. He took out of a drawer of his desk a red leather box, which had copper clips on the outside to close it. In it, were three identical commemorative medals from the 1800's. One was bronze, the other was silver and the third was gold. When he examined the medals again, he remembered that his father had given this box to him many years go, and he did not know the story behind his medals let alone how his father came into possession of them and for what occasion they were struck. Inside the silk lid, was stamped in gold the name Begeer, and that meant that in the attic of the factory, he might find the original dies. He took the medals to the office and asked an expert about the gold content of the gold one. He had a plan. If he could find the die, he could strike one in bronze, have it gold plated and then sell the real gold one and the difference could be spent at the black market for food. A brilliant idea, he thought.

At the office he had the gold one checked. "Where did you get these medals?' the assayer asked. "My father gave them to me a number of years ago", my father answered. "Why did you ask?" After the tests, he said:" You better ask your father to do some explaining, because the gold one is gold plated" "That is impossible", my father said, "He would have told me". Back home he called his father. "You know that red leather box you gave me a number of years ago?" "Did you know that the gold one is gold plated?" "Of course" my grandfather replied, "I remember it well. During the First World War we had a very cold winter and the only way to get coal for the stove was to buy it on the black market, so, then I had a brilliant Idea. If Begeer still had the dies, I could have a bronze one struck and that one gold plated, and then I could sell the gold one back to the company "Sorry, son, but I beat you to it".

During the war, we were all relatively healthy, in spite of the food problems we had to cope with. But one incident landed me in a primitive, makeshift hospital in Leiden. One summer day, I cut my foot on a piece of glass outside. The cut healed quickly, as our doctor cleaned and treated the wound. But while it was healing nicely on the outside, an infection developed inside and went into the blood stream. Then it settled in a cavity near the kidneys where it started to grow until the cavity was filled. It now started to press against the kidneys and a very painful period began. Dr. de Haan, thinking that it was a kidney problem sent me to the hospital in Leiden. Since the regular hospital had to be closed for some reason, a temporary hospital was set up in a missionary school, which was closed as well. I had a high fever, when they carried me up the stairs of the school on a stretcher. I felt every step and turn with agonizing discomfort. Then they carried me into a classroom, which had been used to teach physics and chemistry, because it had a little sink and a water faucet. They gave me painkillers until the doctors decided to continue with something stronger, I was given morphine.

The next day, four doctors were standing around my bed and it was a coincidence that one doctor, a tall one, happened to be a friend of my father. I heard him say to the other three doctors: "I am going to cut it open to see what's wrong". The others said in unison:" I don't want to take any chances" Then the tall one said "If we don't, he will not make it until tomorrow, I am going to take charge". I heard every word and knew that now I was in trouble. Then, when he did, he made only one cut in the affected area and the infected fluids spurted out with a great force, and immediately, my fever dropped to normal. He placed two glass drainage tubes into the wound and then sowed the wound up around them. Then he talked to me when I was awake again. "This is a serious infection, and to completely get rid of it, I will give you an experimental drug. You are the first in the country to receive it and I am not certain about side effects" Please let me know immediately when that would happen. "What is that drug called, doctor?" I asked. "It's called Penicillin" he answered. In a week I was back home and Dr. de Haan visited me at home. "I have good news and I have bad news", he told me. "The bad news is that, while I really tried, I did not get any extra ration stamps for you, but the good news is that I thought of another scheme. We have four soup kitchens in town and I have made arrangements with the organizers that every morning you would act as an inspector, and your job is to go on your bike to each one and "Inspect" the food. Of course to do a really good job a large portion is essential!" I recovered remarkably quickly and when that happened, I was out of a job!

Many people came to my father at the factory with their heirlooms. To buy wedding rings, it was necessary to give the factory the gold needed, because now the gold stock was buried under the flower garden. He was getting these old silver and gold items and at first they landed on his desk. One day, he had a little box, which belonged to a client. In it, pressed in wax were two very large diamonds. A client wanted to have these set in a modern piece of jewelry. But on that day, he was looking for that box, which was nowhere to be seen. He asked around, but to no avail. Then one colleague suggested that he phone a clairvoyant in The Hague. "This is not a joke", my father replied, as he was now getting nervous. But when his colleague insisted, he phoned reluctantly, after he was assured that he had nothing to lose. "Would you please stay on the phone? I have to concentrate", the clairvoyant asked him. Then he said: "You are in a room. I see desks or tables in front of the windows. The windows seem round at the top. You are standing in front of one desk, oh, wait, that's strange, I don't see any windowsills. The desks must be higher than the windowsills. Why don't you lean over the desk and look on the window sill". My father leaned over and then he saw that little box that had fallen off the desk and onto the windowsill. "I found it", my father said enthusiastically, "What do I owe you? "Just send me my normal fee in the mail", was the reply.

A week before the end of the war, Rudolf and I found a metal box, painted in a green military colour, When we opened it we found it contained many chocolate bars and we were immediately very popular as we were generous to a fault. We did not see any chocolate bars at all during the war; they just disappeared. But it created a problem since all the recipients had great trouble falling asleep. It appeared that the box had fallen out of an airplane and the chocolate bars were meant for the crew to keep them awake during those long bombing raids to Germany. They contained Benzedrine to keep them awake.

At long last in May of 1945, the war was over. The Allied troops arrived in Western Holland and we waited in anticipation. A few houses further up the street lived a teenaged girl, who was always dressed in jodhpurs, or riding pants and leather riding boots. Unfortunately there were no horses in Wassenaar anymore as the Germans had made certain of that, but she was dreaming to get on a horse again as soon as possible. She told us many times, that after the war was over, and when the Canadians would come through our street, she would jump on the first jeep, and kiss a real Canadian soldier, and then she would marry the guy. We always had a big laugh about her girlish fantasy; besides, the Canadians might not even come through our street. But then the troops did come through our street and they were Canadians and almost the whole town was present on the sidewalk to greet them. Rudolf, our parents and I were all waiting with little Dutch flags in our hands. When we saw the first jeep in the distance, we looked in the direction of the girl's house and then we saw her running out of the house and jump on a jeep, when it passed her house. When she passed us, she sat crammed between two soldiers, waiving to us and then grabbing one of them. Then all jeeps and trucks drove to the end of the street and then made a right turn towards the highway. Several weeks later she was back. We asked her "What happened, did you marry the guy as you planned?" "Yes, I did, but he was not a Canadian. He was the only Dutch soldier in the group. When this outfit entered the Netherlands in Southern Limburg, he was in the underground and then he joined the Canadian army.

Fourty years later, in Canada, in Saint John, New Brunswick, I met Judge Rodman Logan. He told me that he was planning a visit a special town near The Hague. "Which one?" I asked, "Wassenaar", he answered. We came through that town and we had quite a reception. I was the commander of my unit". "Wassenaar?" I answered "I was standing on the sidewalk , were you perhaps in the first Jeep?" "Of course", he replied, "Then I saw you in 1945 and you must have seen me, because I was waiving my little flag at you". It was a strange coincidence that after emigrating to Canada, I would wind up in New Brunswick from which the Carleton and York Regiment, 3rd Brigade of the 1st Canadian division liberated my home town led by lieutenant Rod Logan. Later, I learned that he had married a Dutch girl himself.

Rudolf was born in Wassenaar and he went to the same elementary school as I and we often biked together, then he went to a different secondary school and after graduating, he worked for Unilever. The company sent him to London to work on advertising for the company. He was very artistic and musical. Played piano as the best and was a favourite at parties everywhere. He painted well and his talents were being noticed at the company. After London they sent him to Paris, and in 1955 he married his Dylia, after a holiday in Switzerland. A son was born in Paris after working for a large, but different company. Then he decided to come back and start his own little company selling promotional articles for companies. Dylia became ill and died and he was left with a son and two daughters. He remarried, which was very fortunate, because he could not stand being alone. He was the real optimist in the family and was able to have a great influence on us all, in particular during the dark days of war.

CHAPTER TEN

HITCHHIKER

After the celebration of our liberation from five years of war, at the end of May, the citizens of the Netherlands were preparing to return to a life they remembered from the good time before the war. They wanted to pick up, where they left off, but they found that that time was now behind them. The country had changed. Many citizens did not remember, they were too young when it all started. I was now nineteen and Rudolf was two years younger. The trains were still not running, there was no gasoline and very few cars were on the road. It took time to have everything normal again. Our houseguests had left and they took the food-for-a-rainy-day with them. My friend Jan's father, next door, went back to his normal routine as a captain of the The Hague police force and his mother was still playing her beloved piano, but I felt that I was cooped up in Wassenaar for so long that I was longing just get out.

One night, a jeep drove up in front of the house and an American military officer stepped out. My parents, Rudolf and I were just sitting at the dinner table when the doorbell rang. The sound still made us a bit edgy, but it turned out to be a friendly visitor, bringing greetings from my uncle Willem in Detroit. My father's younger brother had settled in the United States long before the war. His family now consisted of Aunt Gonda and their daughters Flora, Helen and Gertrude. We occasionally heard from him through the Red Cross and were anxious to hear the latest news. I asked the captain where he would go later, when he joined us for supper. "Paris", he answered. He said the magic word, and I asked him if I could go with him. "Don't ask questions like that", my father said, but the captain interrupted. "No, really, that's fine with me. I have no objections, in fact, I like company, and after all, I have to drive 500 kilometers. That night we drove to Paris, where I was to stay in an army encampment near the university. "You can use the bed of my lieutenant, who is on furlough. And don't worry about the food; I'll give you enough vouchers to eat at the officer's mess. I was free to go where I wanted to go and after a week, I hitchhiked home. Now I had the travel bug, and Jan and I decided to thumb our way back to France together. One morning, we packed our gear and left for LaRoche in Belgium and further to France. Getting rides seemed easy and we had a good idea where we wanted to go. I told Jan that to go to Paris, we had to go straight south. He disagreed. With me, we were let off a cross road and he was standing on one corner and I at another. He soon was able to get a ride, and a bit after I was on the road south. Later in the day, I came out of a van, to get a lift to my next destination, when on the other side, coming from a different direction, Jan stepped out of a truck. We had a good laugh and traveled together again.

Eventually, we wound up in Chamonix at the foot of the Mont Blanc. Our last ride was in a sports car and the driver, we thought, was a maniac, driving as fast as possible over the mountain roads and taking hairpin corners as close as he could get. The ride before, was much more pleasant. It was a taxi and the driver pointed at the groom and bride on the back seat. "C'est un taxi d'amour" he explained.

When we arrived, we checked into a youth hostel and then we dropped our gear in the room. At the hostel, they asked us, if we had mountain boots, ropes and other gear. We didn't have anything of the kind and walking outside, we decided to go up the mountain anyway to feel the ice of the glacier. A French fellow joined us and we we're on our way. The three of us climbed through the woods on a trail leading to the top to the glacier. We noticed something that we had never thought off. We were used to low lands, we did not live near mountains in Holland and now we saw the sun disappearing behind the Mont Blanc. We realized that we had only a small window of opportunity before we had to return to the hostel, but soon we arrived at our destination. The glacier was higher than we thought. The ice came almost to our middle, when we stood beside it. Very big boulders were lodged into the ice here and there and when we looked over the glacier down, we could see the town of Chamonix, quite small. "I am going to climb on one of those boulders to have a better look", I said. The French fellow told me not to take any chances, while Jan said: " You won't get me up there!" I climbed on the ice and onto a rock, which had a flattened top and I thought that it would be quite safe to stand on it. I don't know how it happened, but when I was trying to stand up, I slipped, and fell on the ice. The French fellow told me later on, that he yelled to throw my legs over my shoulder, but there was little chance that I could do that. I was sliding with my head down and it seemed that the town was getting closer. Then for some unexplainable reason, my body slowly started to turn and now, at least my feet were facing down. Then all of a sudden, I came to a stop. My feet had hit another boulder and now I was laying there, shaking, my jacket and pants torn on one side and unable to move. The French fellow and Jan ran down the path and when they reached me, they dragged me off the ice. I tried to stand up, but I couldn't even walk. It was now getting dark, and leaning on the shoulders of my two friends, we started the path down to the hostel. Halfway down, we met a search party from the hostel. They were absolutely furious and within five minutes we learned all the French swear words in the book. I decided from that moment on, that I would never climb a mountain ever again. Soon we left for home. Our cabin fever had mysteriously disappeared. That year I went back to the Amsterdam Typographical School to finish what I started, and which was so seriously interrupted by a railroad strike and other events as a result of the war. It was not until 1946 that I returned to France.

Having been in France twice, I wondered what was behind that attraction for me, but then one day, when my father was remembering, it struck me. He was telling that my grand parents and my parents were in Paris together in a hotel and that my grandfather proclaimed that it was a scandal, that the hotel did not have any Dutch cheese, which became a bit of a joke among our vacationers. But then he told me what happened and then I realized that exactly nine months after their holiday in Paris, I was born. I cannot find any better reason to explain my fondness for that country.

It was late in the summer when I hitchhiked to Bordeaux. My plan was to find a job in one of the wine castles and work in the vineyards. I was by myself this time and planned to have some fun for a change. When I arrived in Bordeaux, and saw on the map St. Emilion, the name of my father's favourite wine, I had a ride to Libourne and then a ride with a gentleman, who was very interested to hear about my plans to work in a vineyard. Then, out of the blue, he asked if I would like to work for him. I was delighted and now he introduced himself to me as Monsieur Couraleau and he lived in Gensac, a small town, not far from Libourne, which had a train station. When we arrived, he introduced me to his wife and his two daughters. He told me, that I could use the spare room. Later, I was called for supper and I had my first taste of what was to come. At the dinner table I did ask for a glass of water. Monsieur Couraleau was puzzled. Then he explained that water was used to wash your hands and not to drink. He had obviously something else in mind. I could not help but noticing, that in spite of his obvious love for wine, his very family name ended with "eau" which is French for water.

After super, he gave me the grand tour of the farm. In a shed, he had a couple of oxcarts, with on top a very large round barrel, open at the top, and made of oak. Then he had a stable with oxen. He explained that he did not produce much wine as most of his production went to the co-op. There they had two huge funnels outside the building, one for red-flesh grapes and the other for the white ones. Some grapes had white flesh but had red skins and they would go in the white funnel. In the height of the harvest, he would hire people from the Basque area of Spain, just over the border and he would always get the same men each year. Now the harvest of the grapes had started and I had to follow the rows together with the Spaniards. They spoke mostly Spanish, but were able to speak French but with a Spanish accent. Even when I tried, I could not avoid to pickup some of their accent. I can still hear the cry of a man with a metal basket on his back. "Panier, Panier". When the man came through our row, we had to fill his basket on his back from the one with grapes we were using. We emptied our basket in the metal one and when his basket was full, he went to the side of the row of vines, climbed the ladder against the barrel, bend over and all the grapes fell into the barrel. At the end of the day, the barrel was full and monsieur Couraleau led the oxen to the Co-op building. There the grapes were dumped into a funnel, they calculated how much was delivered and he would receive payment at the end of the week. When the harvest was over we had a party for everyone. The neighbours were finished the next day, and we had another party there. The neighbours had a real castle and the owner had invited us to his party and again the young wine was flowing all night. The neighbour, who was the Marquis de Mille, decided to throw the biggest party in town. He had music with local musicians playing accordion, we ate, we drank wine and I danced with his wife in one of the bedrooms of the castle, we heard the music there also loud and clear.

I realized that my time was running out. I hated to leave the Couraleau's, who were so nice to me, and I would miss one of his daughters in particular. I decided to stay a few days more and they had no objection. Then a letter arrived from the Department of Defense that I was to report for duty. The next day at the breakfast table Monsieur Couraleau told me that he had bought a train ticket to The Hague at the railway station in Libourne and that I would leave on Saturday. Since they would go to a wedding on that day, they would drop me off at the station. When he did, I said good-bye with a heavy heart. I would never forget this wonderful family. It was well before eleven and I had still a bit more than an hour before the train would leave and I decided to walk around a bit. I picked up my suitcase and walked down the street from the station. Then I heard bicycle bells ringing behind me and when I turned around, I saw two gendarmes on bikes. Now both flanked me and now they were on foot. They asked me where I was going. The answer was not believable to them and they ordered me to follow them to the police station. They were confused. What was this blond fellow with a suitcase and wearing a French beret, doing on Saturday morning in Libourne. Would he be the German prisoner of war, who had fled the road gang working on the main road in town? When we arrived at the office of the police chief, the door was locked behind me. They asked a number of questions, and then I had to show my passport and when they looked into my suitcase, they found a stack of letters from home.

The letters looked like German, the passport could be false, a bottle of wine, dried grapes and a souvenir. A clever disguise, he thought. "Where did you stay?" "We stayed with the Couraleau family". Now the chief was going to phone. "They are not home. Are they are at a wedding" "Do they have relatives?" "Yes, their parents live across the street, but they are at the wedding as well" "Do you know anyone else?" Then I remembered. "Yes, the Marquis de Mille". Now he phoned and in minutes I was free to go then I said to them: "My train leaves in twenty minutes and my suitcase is a mess". In minutes, I was sitting on a bike behind one gendarme and my suitcase was sitting behind the other. With only minutes to spare, I boarded the train and I was off to The Hague, where I would take the yellow streetcar to Wassenaar. In the train there were lots of workers with large twenty liter bottles of wine and it was no accident that I arrived in The Hague in a very happy state. On my arrival, I discovered that I did not have any Dutch money on me to pay the conductor, but then he put a ticket in a little envelope and asked me to give it to a conductor the next time I would take the streetcar. On arriving home my parents had a guest, a French lady, who my father knew from his dealings with French manufacturers of art medals. The lady asked me if I had been in France and I told her that I just came from there. "I know in what area you must have stayed for a little while" "Oh, my father told you, didn't you?" "No he didn't" "How do you know then", I asked, "I rather not tell you" and when I told her that I really wanted to know, she said:" You came from the neighbourhood of Bordeaux, because you speak good French, but with a terrible Spanish accent"

CHAPTER ELEVEN

SOLDIER

On Monday morning, I took the streetcar to The Hague. I was to report to an office at the Department of Defence and when I arrived, I found a big lineup of future soldiers. They were all about my own age and I wondered what it would be like to be in uniform and to be ordered around. When I roamed around France, I was my own boss, free as a bird. After being cooped up for five years, that was the life for me. But now I would be cooped up again and I was not particularly enthusiastic about it. But I was drafted; I did not have any choice. After standing in line with the other boys, joking around, making all kinds of remarks, it was my turn. "What will it be?" the officer asked me. "The army, the navy, or the air force".

Somehow, during my travels, I had lost interest in walking, and I thought, cleverly, I should choose the navy, with the air force as my second choice. After all, how much could you walk on a ship or plane? As a kid, I took part in marches of ten or fifteen kilometer with as prize a medal with a fancy ribbon. I had a number of these somewhere, but the army was no choice it all. As it turned out, that is not the way it works, because they seem to have it in for me as I was drafted into the army. What I did not know at that time was that I was to walk for three years constantly in a tropical heat. Now I really had my marching orders and I was to report to boot camp in a town in the centre of the country and they gave me a one-way train ticket. Now I was officially a soldier and I realized that I better make the best of it but I did felt that I just lost my freedom. I asked how long I was to be in the army, but the answer was not forthcoming.

The next morning, I had to report to the train station to board a special train for the military, and I joined hundreds of would be soldiers on our first day of army life. Ede was a small town with a military camp and a large area set aside for training. Already we learned that the barracks were condemned after the First World War, but may be that was just a rumour. We noticed, that the lights in the rooms were just a wire coming out of the ceiling with one single bulb hanging down and the room was cold. The toilets were out of order and they told us that we had to go outside, where, between the buildings a large underground bunker was built, a leftover from the Second World War. On either side of the bunkers was an opening with three steps down. Inside was a long row of chemical toilets and the place stank. It was late fall and going to the toilet in the middle of the night was not what we would like to do.

At the entrance of the barracks there was a wrought iron fence and a gate, next to which a gatepost, a small building, obviously newly built. Now I was in uniform, and getting used to army life, with reveille, parades, mess breaks, gymnastics and patrols, I was one of the first they selected to stay at watch near the gatepost. This small building had a washroom and a faucet with water, almost all the luxuries of home. And now I had my instructions and wait for the time that someone else would take over, and I could go to bed. Then a car drove up and the driver turned out to be the wife of the commander of the barracks. She asked for her husband, and I phoned him to fetch her. While she was waiting, she asked to go to the washroom. I hailed other soldier and asked him to take the lady to the bunker and stay watch at one of the entrances. Next day, I was to report to the commander, who, at first looked very serious, he pretended to be mad, saying that he could lock me up for that, he could not pretend anymore however and burst out in laughter. "I know, you wanted to tell us that the situation is intolerable, don't worry, we'll do something about it, besides we already had a warning from the Department of Health. As it turned out, luckily, he had a sense of humour.

I gradually made friends and since we were all there together, we might as well have some fun. The problem was that the powers to be did not always have a sense of humour and we were often punished for our pranks. The commander did not overrule the decisions made by the training officers either unfortunately, as he did not want to show his sense of humour to them. One of the soldiers was a very shy fellow and naturally became a target. He slept in a metal bunk bed made from tubing. We stole out of the dispensary a bottle of alcohol, then put corks in the top of the four tubes and when he was sleeping, we filled the tops with alcohol. Then we lit four fires after which we woke him up. It was now getting cold and since the central heating system was out of order, each room had a potbellied stove, a metal pail with coal and kindling wood to start a fire. Most of us slept in wooden bunk beds on straw mattresses. Sometimes, we would take a plank from under our mattresses and we warmed ourselves near the roaring fire. We did that a bit too often, because eventually, most of us were sleeping on not more than three planks, barely enough to hold the mattress. Then, when one soldier left for some reason, his whole bed disappeared. One day, the captain called me in his room. "Today it is your turn to start the stove for me" "But you don't have any kindling wood", I answered, "Why don't you use a plank out of your own bed?" He knew what was going on.

After the initial training, we were allowed to go home for the weekend for the first time. Special trains were coming into the station to handle the traffic. We took our seats eagerly. Outside were waiters dressed in white jackets, holding large serving trays with paper cups, walking alongside the train, pouring coffee out of a large silvery coffee can and collecting money. Knowing that they had only a short period of time, they worked as fast as possible to serve as many soldiers, leaning out of the windows, as possible. Now the train started to move, and they walked and poured faster now. They wanted to get the most out of the opportunity, but now the train was going faster, and when he was close to end of the platform, one soldier grabbed the coffee pot, held his arm outstretched and at the end dropped the pot, landing on a pile of sand.

After a few weeks in uniform, the recruits had undergone a transformation, from civilian to a military, from boy to man and they are now ready to take on the world, at least that is what they thought. By the time my training period was finished, five of us decided not to go home, but cross the border into Germany. We wanted to have one day of fun, before we would go home for a couple of days. With a jeep, which we were allowed to take, we went to the nearest town on the other side of the border and we went to the only bar in town. Since I had never been in a bar myself, I had no idea what to expect. When we entered the building we found ourselves in a long corridor with black painted walls in which pieces of mirror were imbedded and hanging from the ceiling a large ball of light, turning around and giving the hall a spooky feeling. Entering the dimmed lit room, we saw round tables and chairs and at the other end a stage with red curtains both closed. Would they have a stage show, we wondered, and in anticipation the five of us chose the table right in front of the stage, just in case.

Then the room darkened even more and the curtains opened and the music started. The five of us watched for what was to come and then a black girl in a red petticoat came on stage and started dancing to the music. She turned out to be a stripper and first, the top came off, which she nonchalantly dropped on a chair in the corner. Now the five soldiers looked with wide-open eyes. Then the dancer took off her petticoat, swirling it over her head while dancing. Then she stopped and looked at the table with the soldiers in front of the stage and the music was getting louder. "Oh, my God, she is getting off the stage" said one soldier. Now she came down the three steps, still swirling her petticoat over her head and looking us over at the same time. Now she was going around our table and then she looked at me and she noticed that my face had taken the colour of her petticoat, and then she stopped behind my chair and placed the petticoat around my neck and on my shoulders. The other boys roared with laughter. After having a couple of beers, we returned the jeep, went to the station and boarded a train to go home. The following week we were again to report to our units, but we had no idea what was in store for us.

After a week's holiday, I was to report to the military academy in the city of Breda. Not that I had any interest in becoming a professional soldier, but then, it was not my choice to make. This period was of very short duration. The situation in the Netherlands Indies became very serious. Local political groups there, were looking for independence, and would do anything to achieve that. But in our country, the powers to be were planning not to give up without a fight and we were selected to do the fighting. I was sent home for a long weekend and then I had to report in a town in the centre of the country. It was a cold November day in 1946, that my parents brought me to a military camp and to say good-bye.

It was a year after entering the army and now I was promoted to corporal and I was not a recruit anymore. From that camp we were brought to Rotterdam Harbour. A Passenger liner, the SS Nieuw Holland, was converted to a troop transport ship. It still had all the trappings of a cruise ship, but we did not sleep in cabins, as they were reserved for the officers. We slept in hammocks, in the halls, in the gym and other places. The voyage was uneventful and we started to get lessons in Malay, which was not a difficult language to learn. When we passed the equator, they had a large tarpaulin strung up on deck as we were going to be baptized by King Neptune. They threw us in the water filled tarpaulin and with wooden swords we were getting a pretend shave after which we were given a certificate, signed by King Neptune himself, stating that we had passed the equator for the first time. We sailed through the Suez Canal and in Suez, a man with a fez on his head boarded ship. He was a magician, who traveled from Suez to Port Said and would return on another ship back home. He made chicks disappear under big metal cups. Local kids were inviting us to throw money overboard so they could dive for the coins. Merchants in rowboats were selling their wares and a basket on a rope was used to exchange goods for money when we went through the Red Sea. We saw camels in the desert, we were passing tankers and sometimes we had to enter a wider piece of the canal to let other ships pass. It was getting much warmer now, although at night a cool wind would blow from the desert. We knew that we would be having our last bit of fun on this cruise ship and that on arrival in the Netherlands Indies, reality would set in.

It was hot below deck. We waited in our hammocks for our next meal and since I had the second shift, I decided to walk around. I passed an area with a little shop and in one, behind the counter was a civilian sitting on a chair. He did not look so good and I asked him "what's the matter?" then he told me that he was seasick. "It must be your first trip" I added "Not at all" he replied. I am at sea for twenty years and every trip I am seasick for the first four or five hours." I found that strange, I wished him the best and I went upstairs to eat. The poor fellow was a member of the crew. During the voyage we had nothing better to do than play cards or other games or see a movie and when we were a couple of days from arriving in Batavia, we had to listen to lectures from our officers, about what to expect, how to behave and what we can and shouldn't eat.

Batavia was the capital of the Netherlands-Indies and it looked more like a town than a city. No high rise, hardly any traffic and fishing boats, called prauws in the harbour. Now, so many years later, the city is called Jakarta, the capital of Indonesia, with high apartment buildings and large office towers, with cars and trucks and trains and large ships in the harbour. The City's population had exploded. To recall our lives in the tropics is hard, but when I look at the black and white photo's I took and look into the regimental history book we received after our return, a number of events are coming back into my memory. Some pages are devoted to pictures of those who died. Those gave me painful memories, because most of these soldiers I knew I had lived with and I saw death in the worst possible way. They appeared so young in my book and then I realized that I too was the same age, yet in those three years, I never had a scratch and for a few years after my return, I had guild feelings about that. From my company, I counted twelve soldiers. They were friends, thrown together by fate, sharing life together and while it is hard and often exhausting, we also had fun, whenever that was possible. Sure, I had a kidney stone and since we drank a lot in the tropics, it disappeared. I also had malaria, but bitter quinine pills solved that problem. Some died due to an accident, but most were killed in action. The enemy were not very well armed at the time, but still gave us a great deal of resistance. Posters with "Merdeka" (Freedom) were everywhere and on the walls were painted in the Malay language:" If the Dutch soldiers enter your village, don't be afraid. Beat your drums and warn us. We will take care of them".

One day, Corporal Ger Christian had placed his jeep on a self made ramp to give it a thorough cleaning after a day's run in the country. He placed a pail of gasoline on the ramp in which he had poured some oil. It was a perfect combination. He dipped his rag in the mixture and washed the jeep. The gasoline would evaporate and a thin layer of oil made the jeep look new. For some unknown reason the gasoline in the pail caught fire and he tried to escape, but was unable to. He burned to death. Another time I saw another soldier running out of a building. He was a butcher and while cutting a large piece of meat, his knife slipped and went into his stomach. He ran, to get help, but he was bleeding so profusely, that I saw him fall and die.

Every night we were cleaning our weapons, sitting around a table. One soldier, thinking that the chamber was empty, clicked the trigger and killed the boy across from him. These experiences during the first three months of being in a strange land, made us decide that going to the tropics was not a vacation anymore and the reality was setting in. Now, when we were on patrol, and when we were shot at, we had to protect ourselves at all times and I wondered if I would have been safer on a ship or in an airplane far away from this place. The enemy had found a large cache of large bombs near the airport, a leftover from the Second World War by the Japanese Air Force.

The Japanese occupied the country at the time. The bombs were removed and they used them to bury these bombs under the sandy roads. Only in the city roads were paved at the time. If we saw signs that the road had been dug up, we usually stopped. The truck drivers always had a passenger with binoculars, just for this reason. But it was not always detectable and when our trucks, jeeps and other vehicles drove over the area, people were waiting in the bushes with a rope in their hands, then, with a firm tug, an explosion occurred usually under a truck, carrying many solders. That happened many times and since we never drove alone, always a number of vehicles at a time, many of us had to deal emotionally with the result. Many soldiers were killed that way, but strangely enough, the truck or jeep I was in, was never hit.

Sometimes, we had to sweep a forest, where we thought the enemy was waiting for us in holes in the ground. We would go through the whole forest forming a wide line of armed soldiers and when we reached the end of the woods, we were being shot from behind. What did we miss? Where did they come from? Did they bury themselves somewhere? Looking in my photo album, I see eighteen men in front of a hut. They look a rowdy lot to be sure. No shirts, some wearing a hat or a helmet, sandbags in front of the hut for protection and a little brown boy, kneeling in front of the troops. Each platoon had a Djongos, or boy, assigned to it to do chores around the camp. A native woman in a sarong, called a baboe, would do the laundry and the cooking. This was not at all the army life we had at home.

Returning from a long patrol tired and hungry, carrying rifles, a bren gun or a sten gun, a shower and a good meal was all that was needed to bring us back to civilization. The shower was usually near a well consisting of a metal pail on a rope and cool water to wash off the sweat of the day. One day, we decided to set a hut on fire. We had a hunch that the hut was used to store ammunition. As it turned out, the bamboo hut was filled with bullets concealed in the hollowed bambo stems and under the earthen floor was a bomb, buried for later use. The fire caused fireworks with bullets flying around in all directions and then there was an enormous explosion. We were right and we were also lucky that nobody was hurt.

We had two clergymen assigned to us. One was a Jesuit priest and the other a protestant minister. They shared a jeep. The minister was armed with a pistol, but the priest refused to carry a gun. One day they wanted to go to the front line together, but were refused permission. They felt that they were needed there more than on the other side of the line. In that area heavy fighting was going on. The commander was insisting, but they decided to go anyway. Within the danger zone the jeep struck a mine. The priest was thrown clear of the jeep but the minister was hurt and was hit in his leg. Immediately a soldier and I were assigned to carry him out of the danger zone on a stretcher. We also had to walk, because the vehicles present could not be missed. Little did we know that we had to carry him almost three kilometers before we could bring him to safety and where he could get help. He was six feet tall and that made it hard slugging in the heat. We did not encounter any problems along the way, which was a relief. After some weeks, he was sent home with a decoration and three years later, back home in Wassenaar, I saw him standing in the backyard next door. "What are you doing here?" I asked him, "I live here", he answered, and then I said: " what do you know, so do I".

One day, we went to the island of Madura, east of Surabaja, Java. For the first time we were using a landing craft. We were all nervous, because we did not know what was waiting for us. On the way, we suddenly heard a shot and were ready to respond, but later we learned that one soldier's sleeve had been caught in the trigger of his bren gun. Then all of a sudden, we were all told to get ready to leave the craft. "Grab your gear and your weapons and make certain, that you keep your gun in the air, because we are going into the water. We were looking at the coast nearby and we noticed people walking on a dike. Then one lit a flashlight towards us and the lieutenant told us that the advance mining crew was already hard at work and it was the signal he was waiting for. It was now 2:30 in the morning and we felt a shock, when the bottom of the boat hit the sand. The water must have been shallow, we thought.

We heard the distant talk of the mine clearing crew and then we heard the engine of a bulldozer, driving towards the beach. Then our boat dropped its front panel into the water and we were ready to leave the boat. Walking carefully, in the dark, carrying our rifle in the air, we held on to the side, then stepped out and found ourselves to our middle in cold sea-water. Our ammunition bags on our belt were now full of salty seawater. We were shivering and that really woke us up. Our clothing cringed to our bodies, when we stepped on land. We felt kilo's heavier, and then we felt the water running out of our jackets and pants, into our boots. We felt better, having solid ground under our feet. Good thing, out ammunition bags had grommet holes at the bottom, the water just poured out. We climbed onto the dike and sat down behind it, to get a rest. It was getting light at the horizon, when we heard a heavy splash behind us, on the other side of the dike. A bren-gunner and his assistant had just stepped out of a landing craft and onto a rock. The rock tipped and both fell into the water.

First to come up was the assistant and we heard him saying: "Frig, now the photo of my girlfriend is all wet". A minute later the bren-gunner came up, still holding on to his gun. Now the two made their way to the beach. In the meantime, we watched the mine crew lift a large saucer shaped mine out of the ground and we were all told to drop down and take cover. After a while our clothing had dried out in the hot sun and now, because if the heat, we were getting wet again. It was noon, when we entered the village, which seemed deserted. We set up watch posts and then the rest of us were told to get some rest. Our patrol made a quick sweep after our rest and all seemed secure, when all of a sudden local people with their thumbs up into the air came out of the woods. We asked for something to drink and then the residents brought us bananas, papayas and Chinese pears as well. Now, in the distance, we saw large clouds of smoke and we heard explosions. The Republican army was probably blowing everything up, waiting for our arrival. We saw large numbers of people with thumbs in the air and some Chinese carrying a large Chinese flag. These people were skinny and hardly had any clothes on and their feet were bare.

Just before entering the town of Bankalan, we stopped at the police barracks. Those were the only buildings still standing, as all other buildings had been blown up or were still burning. The bridge in town had been blown up. We were taking another route and arrived at the town square, where the amtracks were set up with guns pointing in all directions. The Marines had set up their vehicles as well and were busy setting up camp. At last we could relax. Behind barbed wire and sand bags we felt safe, but we knew that it was only temporary. The next day, our regular job began. From our post in Bankalan, we started our daily and nightly patrols of the whole area. We were shot from buildings, from trees and palm trees and from bushes. When that happened, we acted quickly. Response was not always easy as we seldom saw those who were shooting at us. Then one day, the worst happened. A soldier was hit and died instantly. We were not prepared for this and then we thought, that we might be next. Capturing the island, one section at a time, we were to find out, that the enemy was stronger than we thought.

We were a full year on Madura, that little island east of Java. It was a pleasant place and during the rainy season, we had a cease-fire. On Parade, one day we were given decorations and honored the 43 soldiers we had lost. In that period we had it finally easy. We were supplied with canned potatoes and canned meat, too often, and we were eager to eat something else instead of soldier's grub. We decided to go into the village to see if we could trade our canned goods for chickens. We took a dozen cans of pork with us, cans clearly marked with a pig's head on the label. The man was excited about the trade and we came to a deal. The man grabbed the cans and then I took one back from him. "You are not allowed to eat this meat", knowing that he was a Muslim. The man dropped all the cans on the ground, sat down and began to rip all the labels off the cans. "Now my wife does not know what meat that is, " he said. Talking to the man gave us the feeling that those people felt secure among us. Thinking back, our best time was during the cease-fire. The only problem was that I became bored and when I heard that the driver of a mobile canteen needed a helper to follow the troops, I applied and got the job. We drove all around East Java and Madura and I was sitting at the back, next to the pop- and coffee machines, looking out of the open back and taking in the view from a lazy chair.

Wherever we went, we were supplied with beds for the night and I felt that I had struck the lottery. But then, a problem arose. The roof of the truck was leaking and water went into the merchandise and then we were ordered to go to Surabaya to wait for a replacement truck. I actually had a holiday of sorts and at night I took in a movie at the cinema, mostly Chinese with Malay subtitles. One night an officer sat in front of me and, turning around, asked me who I was and what I was doing in the cinema. I told him and then he ordered me to return to Madura immediately. Lying on a thick load of bedding in a three-ton open truck, I reluctantly returned and went back to my unit to report for duty.

After two years, we were due for some recreation and a holiday. We were sent to a famous resort in East Java. It had an Olympic sized swimming pool and we called it "The Oasis". We could not believe our luck. On arrival we were ready to settle in and have a swim, when, all of a sudden, we were told that we would have a curfew until further notice, because the enemy had surrounded the resort. They told us that 4,000 heavily armed men were waiting to attack. Since the resort had little protection, we were in a very difficult situation. Five of us volunteered to get help and in the middle of the night, we went past enemy posts to go to a nearby village, were a company of the artillery was stationed. This holiday turned out to be a bust. We never did get a chance to swim. Then we went back to Madura. The cease-fire ended and the fighting started all over again and after the western part of the island was captured, we controlled the whole island ourselves, because the engineers, the Marines and minesweeping crews had left for the mainland and Surabaya. The residents started to rebuild their lives again, while the island was in Dutch hands for now. During the three years in the tropics we had many activities and stayed the longest on the island of Madura. This guerilla war had periods of cease-fire, and then the fighting started all over again.

At last, after three years, we were sent home. Netherlands Indies had become Indonesia and now we boarded a ship from Surabaya to Djakarta (formerly Batavia) and from there we would board another ship to go home. On our arrival in Djakarta, we asked if our next ship home had arrived yet and then we were given the bad news. We were going to have to stay at least two more weeks in the barracks on orders from the Defense department in The Hague. The powers to be there felt, that if we would arrive in Rotterdam harbour, on crutches, in wheelchairs and with casts on our legs and arms, and bandaged heads, it would be bad for public relations. We needed rest, lots of food and our appearance in Holland was to be as good as humanly possible. We eventually boarded the SS Waterman and after the voyage we arrived in Rotterdam and still a large number of soldiers came home on crutches.

A bus brought us to Wassenaar. Rudolf had made a large welcome sign over the entrance of the driveway and my father and mother, Rudolf and Flory, along with her little sons were all there to greet me. I was happy to be home again. The same week, I was to go to the town hall, in the same room, were Flory and Jo were married during the war; I and a number of other soldiers were given engraved crystal drinking glasses with the crest of the town and an inscription. I took my glass to Canada where I displayed it proudly for a number of years. Lydie, then my wife, was not to touch this glass because I was worried that it would get damaged. It was my prized possession. One day, I took it out of the glass cupboard to show it to friends and for the time being, I placed it on the windowsill. Two small sliding windows flanked our front window and since it was summer, these windows were open. Then a truck passed by and one window came crashing down on my precious glass. The Lydie cried out: "Thank God!" For her it was a relief, but for me, it was the end of my army days.

I returned to the Amsterdam Typographical School again to finish my studies and I had decided to immigrate to Canada, where this might be very useful, as I needed to find myself a job. At the same time Uncle Willem and Aunt Gonda visited the family and I had the opportunity to ask him to be on the look out for me, as Detroit was very close to the Canadian border. He told me that he had a friend in Chatham, Ontario, who had a printing shop, and he would talk to him. He did talk to him eventually, but I was not aware how that would change my life on the first day in Canada.

CHAPTER TWELVE

BECOMING A SETTLER

They all were to see me off at Rotterdam Harbour. My father Armold, my mother Ies, my two bothers, Jaap and Rudolf and my sister Flory, who was with her husband Dr. Jo Bok. They were allowed to go right to the gangplank, and while waiting, we talked about Canada and what was waiting for me there. The ship was loaded with supplies for the voyage and while we were watching, they all asked questions. "Do you have your passport and your tickets? "What about your boarding pass?". Then Jo asked: "Do you have enough money?" I had to admit, it wasn't much. I had 15 American dollars, in cash, 15 Canadian dollars in cash, and 170 dollars in Travelers Cheques. But I had a ticket to New York, a train ticket from Pennsylvania station to Chatham, Ontario, a job waiting there and an employer offering me to put me up until my first pay cheque." Then Jo said: "I had in my desk an American 100 dollar bill which was a left over from a trip to a medical convention some years ago, here take that with you". I thanked him; I was certain that it might come in handy someday.

Then it was time to cross the gangplank to a new adventure. I took my suitcase and holding my boarding pass in my other hand and went on board. I stayed on deck to wave my family good bye and then the ship, now loose from its moorings, left for America. I waited a while, seeing the family getting smaller and waived again and went looking for my cabin. There was something familiar about this ship, and then I realized that this must be a sister ship of the one I went to the Indies with, but this one was still different. Now I was getting a real cabin. I did not have to sleep in a hammock anymore. When I left, it was mid-April and

Holland was greening. The tulips were out and the trees were getting green and the bulb fields near my home were now in full bloom. Now I started to wonder if I had done the right thing. Would Canada be under a blanket of snow or would it be spring there as well. I noticed that a lot of emigrants were on board. They told me that in Le Havre, a Frenchman would come on board and would join me in my cabin. Then I met a very skinny German with a dark voice and a very large moustache. He had an accordion and all he did all day was playing that instrument and singing very sentimental German songs. There was quite a mixture of nationalities on board; Frenchmen, Americans, Englishmen, Belgian and German settlers; and at the dinner table you heard all these languages spoken at the same time.

It was early in the morning, when our ship docked in New York. I was still asleep. When I awoke, I looked out of my porthole, to watch the activities outside and I decided to get off the ship and have a look around. Breakfast was not for another half hour or so, and I wanted to explore a bit. We were docked in front of a large building and forklift trucks were busy taking loads off the ship. They were driving in and out of the building. I walked to the end of the building and near the corner, I noticed some men hunched down and others standing behind as if they were waiting for something. Two men in the middle, held a large wooden crate a foot off the ground, one corner of which was pointed to the concrete floor below. Then they dropped the crate hitting the concrete and now all the men were taking turns filling flasks from a stream of yellow liquid coming out of the corner of the crate.

I had a day to kill in New York and on top of the Empire State building I discovered a machine, which could record a message on a small gramophone record. Later I mailed my message to my parents. Then at nightfall, I went to Pennsylvania station to take the train to Canada. It was still dark, when the conductor woke me up. "Chatham is our next stop", he said. "Impossible" I said, "It is still dark outside and it will be light when I arrive in Chatham, Ontario, in Canada". "No," he said, "Your ticket is for Chatham, New York". What should I do. "You have two choices", the conductor said, "Either you get off the train in Chatham here or you pay extra and you can stay in the train to Chatham in Canada".

"How much would that cost", I wondered. "Eighty dollars American", he said, and I handed the $100 bill that I had received from my brother in law, Jo, to the conductor.

When I arrived in Chatham, it was light and the sun was shining bright. I left the railroad station with my suitcase in hand and looked around. "So, this is Canada", I thought, "It certainly looks different". I looked at the address on the letter, and I found the home of the owner of Mercury Press, the printer, who had signed my papers and who was the friend of uncle William. I rang the bell, full of anticipation and after a while, the door opened. The printer stood in the door opening in his housecoat, slippers and holding a newspaper in his hand. He seemed friendly enough, but did not invite me in. I showed him my letter, and then he told me that he did not had a job for me and I certainly could not stay there, because his mother-in-law was coming to stay a while. He only signed those papers to help his friend in Detroit and never expected that I actually would wind up on his doorstep. He wished me well, however, and closed the door on me.

For a first time in Canada, I was not impressed. I picked up my suitcase and wondered what to do. I realized that I did not know a living soul in the whole of Canada and I was thinking that the only place I might go is to a police station and ask for advice.

There, a big burly police sergeant put me at ease and invited me behind the counter, "Sit down, get a load off your feet", he said. "Do you have any relatives here?" he asked, "Not here, but I do in Detroit, Michigan". I did not want to go to America. "My plan was to stay here in Canada" I answered. "Did you have lunch yet?" I shook my head. He grabbed the phone and I heard him saying on the phone to someone to bring in a hamburger and a coke. "It is getting a bit late do something about this, why don't you stay here for the night?", he asked "Where?", I wanted to know, then he turned his back and pointed to an open door. "In jail?" I asked,

"Don't worry, we leave the door open" "Tomorrow we'll see what we can do for you.

Early in the morning the sergeant woke me up. "Get up", he said, "I have some news for you". As it turned out a pea cannery needed a time keeper and he was certain that I could do that job and his brother's neighbours had a boarding house and the owner was willing to take me in and I did not have to pay until I received my first pay cheque.

This was the beginning of my life in Canada and I still remember the first day, when I slept in a holding cell at a police station.

Now I was in Canada, but still my thoughts were at home at times. I thought of Rudolf, the brother I grew up with. When he was in kindergarten, he had to go to bed at 7.30 at the latest, because Jaap and Flory had to do their homework. Mother loved him extra, because she was proud that at age 41 she had produced such a sunny kid. I was two years older than my brother and we grew up together and Flory and Jaap, called us "the little ones". They went to school in Leiden and we did not see much of them. Before we moved to the Prinsenweg, we lived for a while on the outskirts of the town, and at the back of our home was a farm, where Rudolf was so called helping the farmer. When he was eight, he went to a florist to buy some flowers for his mother's birthday, but he had only 15 cents in his pocket. The florist, who was touched, knew the family very well and gave him a nice bouquet to give to his mother. He played the piano well, and at parties at school, he was always the centre of attention. He was very artistic and was able to paint surprisingly well.

He also had a talent for business, which was not common in our family. Once, during the war, he drove his bicycle to a farm to trade some silver articles for potatoes and he was very successful. Now, since we grew up together, it was for the first time in my life that I was thinking, that I missed him.

Six months after my adventurous arrival in Chatham, my father, in Holland, met his friend Jan Kessler, who was head of a Children's Aid organization in The Hague and he told him that one of his social workers, Lydie van der Kolk, was leaving for Canada. Her older brother Ger, who settled right after the war, had marital problems. His wife had left him and he was left with his little son Onno. He asked his sister, if she could come over for a month of six to look after him, while he would try to get his life together somehow. Mr. Kessler lived in the Kieviet Park and my father knew him for years. He asked his friend if he thought that she would be willing to take with her a small gift for his son who had settled to Canada in the spring. When Lydie left the harbour of Rotterdam with the SS Prins Alexander, she did not have any idea that this little parcel would be an important factor and would change her life completely. It was November when Lydie left for Halifax, Nova Scotia, and her father, who had the flu at the time, had been given strong medicine to enable him to see his daughter off. Lydie's parents watched while tugboats pulled the ship out of the harbour.

A heavy fog covered the water and the visibility was very poor. A small tanker was sailing across the bow of the ship and the captain did not notice the tugboat or the passenger liner. Minutes later, the tanker was hit broad-side by a ship five times its size and overturned. Lydie saw a man wearing a sailor's cap in the water, his arms outstretched, as he disappeared. Later, the tanker sank. This was the beginning of an eventful stage in her life, but she was on a mission, and she was determined to help her brother in his predicament.

When Lydie arrived in Halifax at the now infamous Pier 21, she went to the railroad station to take the train to Toronto, where her brother and little nephew lived. The train to Montreal was full of emigrants and the train was cold. The heating system did not work and the doors did not close properly. She did not sleep at all that night and arrived in Montreal in less than top condition. After this two-day trip, she arrived in Toronto, where her brother Ger and his son Onno picked her up from Union station. Her brother lived in the Northern outskirts of the city and after arriving, she took up her duties as soon as she had settled in. It took two weeks, before she had a chance to go downtown to look me up. She had telephoned to tell me, that she was on her way. When she arrived downtown by city bus, she had no problem finding the Henry street South of College Street and we met for the first time. The street where I lived was full of comfortable two storey houses in the style of the thirties, with covered porches at the front and each one could be a clone of the neighbour's.

At the end of the street was an Orthodox synagogue and on the other side of which was a Jewish bakeshop and a kosher butcher. I often walked past the synagogue and on the steps I saw bearded rabbis with big black hats, sitting on the steps, telling each other the latest gossip, or discussing serious subjects. Their long hair was partly curled around their ears and they were also watching small children playing outside, all wearing skullcaps. One thing I noticed very early when I arrived there to live, that the street signs were in two languages, English and in Hebrew.

My landlord, Ben Schneiderman was a carpenter by trade and his wife was a very kindhearted woman as was her husband. They spoke Polish to each other but to me they spoke English. One day, coming home from work, I found a little dish with a dessert on my night table. She often left me treats. When I finished, I washed the plate in the kitchen sink, and not knowing where to put it, I placed the plate in the refrigerator. I was not aware that in the fridge, Mrs. Schneiderman had reserved two shelves, one for meat and the other for dairy items. I put the dish on the meat shelf and when I was in the kitchen again later, I saw the dish in the garbage pail. I was shocked, but then my landlady explained why she had to do that. It was part of their religion. When Lydie visited me, we talked at length and she told me about her social work background and about her family and she told me about her brother and his experiences in the war. He worked for an automobile agency and his work hours were very irregular and he found himself in a very difficult position.

Her visit was the beginning of my many visits to her new home, and we were seeing a lot of each other and after a while, Lydie decided to stay in Canada. Now she was also able to take a job at the welfare office since her social work background was a great benefit to her employer. I was working at the time at the Toronto Star, and we both took and extra hour off at lunchtime and we both went to City hall to register for our upcoming marriage. This was still in the old city hall that now stands next to a new one, with its modern design. When we entered the building, we saw that we had to go upstairs and we took one of the two curved stairways and at the top, we saw a sign leading us to the right. A small office, with outside the door was a little slanted desk attached to the wall, with forms and a pen on a string. We filled in the form, knocked on the door and entered the room. A man was sitting behind a large desk, almost filling the room. He was having his lunch. He had an open lunch pail on his desk next to a thermos bottle.

With his hand he indicated for us to come in and take a chair. He took another bite of his bread, then a drink from the coffee. He opened the drawer of his desk, put more bread in his mouth, hauled out, what looked like a bible, grabbed our hands and placed these on the book and mumbled something inaudible due to the fact that his mouth was full. Then he took his stamp and put a few stamps on the paper and with one hand he showed us the door. We walked out, rather puzzled, back to the stairs and started to descent. Half way, I stopped, turned around, and asked the question that puzzled both of us the most. "Are we married now?". In October, Lydie went back to Holland with the intention to meet my family. Unfortunately, I could not go with her, because I could not get off from work.

After arriving in Holland, she met the family and was welcomed by all members. She had one anxious moment, however. Father's younger sister, Theo the Lange, wife of an art dealer in Amsterdam, was known for her opinions, which only consisted of either black or white. She either loved a person very, very much, or she could not stand the person, and if that happened, she was almost impossible to endure. With a heavy heart, she took the train to Amsterdam to meet her. She should not have worried. She was so supportive, and enthusiast about her, that nothing could go wrong anymore. After her visit, she took a small ship the MS. Alexandria back to Canada, the ship was calling on London, St. John's, St. Pierre and Miquelon and Quebec and Montreal and there she took the train back to Toronto.

She was free to start a new life in her new country and she was ready to get married as well. It was raining hard when the new bride stepped into the church chapel. People present were Ger and little Onno, Aunt Gonda from Royal Oak, Michigan, and her daughter Helen. The minister told us, that we needed one more witness, before we could proceed. Lydie called her office, and one colleague was prepared to come over to the church immediately. Her Hungarian friend Maria Gyorgy arrived in twenty minutes, and the wedding could begin. After the wedding we all went to our one room apartment, had something to drink and eat, and the guests left. Lydie went back to her social work, and I to my office. After a while, I was offered a job in Oshawa, at the Oshawa daily Times Gazette, and because of that fact, we moved to that town. We rented a cottage and I started to work for a newspaper, but not as a journalist, because my expertise obtained at the Amsterdam Typographical School was more needed than the position of Journalist. Sometimes I was sent out to an errand and one day, the editor asked me to go the Toronto airport to pick up Lord Thompson, who owned the paper, one of many. "And take our beginning reporter with you." he said. So we went to the airport to pick up Lord Thompson of Fleet. He had arrived from England. I was driving the car back to Oshawa and Mr. Thompson and this young reporter sat on the back seat. I listened with interest to the conversation. "How was your flight, Mr. Thompson?" "Fine", he answered. "I wonder what it is like flying first class or business class", the young reporter said out loud. "Young man", Mr. Thompson answered, "Let me give you an important lesson" "I fly only tourist class and all the way from London, I was thinking how much money I saved". "This man", the young reporter must have thought, "owns five hundred newspapers". But then, I was thinking about our own paper. The front hall was nice, with a little table and comfortable chairs and a vase of flowers. It also had a door with milky shaded glass and the words "Employees Only" on the door. Behind the door were linotype machines and they had seen better days, as they were obtained from other papers, now closed. The operators were sitting on chairs in front of the machines and the chairs were held together with chicken wire.

The first years in Canada were difficult, because of rampant unemployment. During that time, we had two sons close apart. Alan was born in 1955 and Brian in 1956 and our lives would become very complicated. When Alan was born, we lived in Oshawa and a year later, when we lived in Belleville, Brian was born. He seemed a healthy baby and as young parents we were elated. Our life was changing, however, as now we had to look after our two siblings, but it became obvious that we were not prepared for what was to come. The baby was standing in his box, but had trouble getting up or taking a few steps and over time it became obvious that walking alone was not happening. Times had changed. The economy in the country was down and the employees needed to keep the company afloat were losing their jobs. and getting a job, any job, was almost impossible.

The only job I could get was at a construction site near Barry, up north, where a mine was opening up. They had built barracks, here the employees would sleep from Sunday night until Friday 5 P.M., and a company bus would take them to Toronto, and pick them up again, when it was time. This was a very low point in our lives and Lydie hated to be alone in the house with the kids. I was a carpenter's helper, and we had metal barrels, where scrap wood was being burned outside, which we used to warm ourselves. On my jacket was a badge with the name of the company, Economy Construction and my number was 391. I still have that badge to remind me, what we have to do in dire circumstances. Meanwhile, we received letters from home, to return, at least for the time being as life in Holland was quite good there. We decided to pack up and fly back, when we received an offer from my parents to stay with them, until I could get a job. We found out that we were considered "returning emigrants" while our kids had the Canadian nationality, although they were listed on my passport as having a Dutch one as well.

I was able to get a job quite soon, and after a while, we moved into a townhouse a few streets behind our family home, towards the centre of town. It was one of those turns in our lives and another one in our unexpected journey.

CHAPTER THIRTEEN

INTERMISSION

We arrived in Holland in mid June 1957. We were really not planning to stay in Holland forever, because, we thought, that when the economy would be better, we would be back in Canada. Besides, we had another powerful incentive. Having a baby with a medical problem, made it essential, that we should return, because in Canada, we had Medicare and in Holland we did not have any chance of being protected from financial ruin, due to medical problems. I did manage to have a couple of jobs during our three-year intermission. The first job was selling Dictaphone dictation systems to large companies. It was not my choice, but under the circumstances, I took what I could get. The idea was, to place a system with a company for a few weeks, and if the management liked it, we had a sale. The problem was that girls, taking dictation with shorthand, did not like the machines and they were sticking hairpins in them as a form of sabotage. Then one sales man had the name of Blaauw. I asked him if he was related to the wife of my cousin, the Radar man, and he was, in fact he was the son of his wife Olga by a previous marriage. He had an uncle who owned the newest model Mercedes Benz. It was a luxury model, and, since he drove a Volkswagen bug, he was anxious to try this car out on the highway.

His uncle let him do that and when he returned, his uncle said, that if he ever would die, he would leave the car to him. He did not believe that it would ever happen, but thought that it was a nice gesture. Two months later his uncle had a heart attack and died. To his amazement a lawyer phoned him that he now was the owner of his uncle's car. He drove his new possession to his office, and the owner of the company, standing in front of the window of his office on the second floor phoned his secretary, telling her that he wanted to talk to his salesman. When he entered the room, the owner asked him: "I hope you are not planning to take that car to our clients, because I would not let you. Our clients would think we are making a killing selling these machines. You better take your Volkswagen bug to go to our clients". I did not really like my job and when I received an offer to work with a Public Relations firm in The Hague, I took it right away.

This was right up my alley and part of the run of the mill work, like writing press releases and other activities, I was given a couple of assignments, which I had to organize from beginning to end, because everyone else in the office was too busy to help me. The first was the arrival of Sir Myer Galpern, the first Jewish Lord Provost of Glasgow. Lord Provost is the Scottish name for Mayor. He represented the Scottish Board of Trade and came for trade talks. I had to pick him up from the airport, organize a press conference in a large Amsterdam hotel and afterwards a reception, for which I had to order wine and cheese, in another room of the hotel. I was standing in front of the window at the airport and the door of the airplane opened and I saw a little man with black hair coming down the stairs. He wore his chain of office, but it was too large for his posture and the picture was too funny to describe. He was followed by three very tall women, one with black hair and two with blonde hair. Obviously his wife and two daughters, I thought. The room with the wine and cheese was waiting and the large room with the press was ready for the press conference.

Beforehand I had the forethought of hiring a piper, which I found amazingly in The Hague. When the press conference lasted longer than planned, I was getting anxious and I asked the piper to start piping in front of the closed doors and the result was that the conference ended. Later in the week I had to arrange for a banquet and I also had to design menus and name cards for the table. When I received a list of the people invited, I was in a panic, because I had no idea about table settings and protocol. Where do you sit a Mayor, a General, a bishop, a professor or a captain of industry? Etiquette is strict and had to be followed to the letter. One cry for help and the information was faxed to the hotel for me immediately. At the wine and cheese party, the Lord Provost had brought with him a large wheel of Scottish Dunlop cheese, and that defeated my intention to promote Dutch cheeses a bit, but otherwise everything went smoothly.

The other assignment was a bit different. This time it was the arrival of Prince Bertil of Sweden. He came to open an exhibition of Swedish products in Rotterdam, each with a beautiful modern design. Again, I had to arrange for him to be picked up from the airport and this time I learned beforehand, that he was totally fascinated by cars and I decided to borrow the newest model Mercedes Benz, hired an uniformed chauffeur and he was picked up in style with a number of cars following him, with members of the Board of Trade, and some other dignitaries. I went to the airport to check if everything went as planned and when I was satisfied that nothing could go wrong, I left for the hotel and waited for them. I was waiting in the lobby, standing in front of a big window and the Swedish ambassador was standing next to me. Then I saw cars coming and stopping in front of the hotel, but not my beautiful Mercedes. I was getting nervous, "Would something have happened?" "Where can he be?" The ambassador guessed my thoughts and said. "Oh, no, he did it again, I should have warned you, I'm sorry". Then he told me what probably had happened.

As soon, his car was outside the airport area and on the big highway, he told the chauffeur to stop and move over. Then he took the wheel and drove the car to Rotterdam and back, trying to find out how fast this car could go. He was not stopped either because nobody could go as fast as he was or he was very lucky. When he did arrive and came into the lobby, he walked over to where I was standing and apologized to me profusely. At the end of the week he left and I was not involved further, and a few days afterwards, I was called to the Swedish embassy and was led into the office of the ambassador, who gave me a bottle of champagne, all wrapped and decorated with ribbons. "His Highness asked me to give this to you", he said.

Less than a month later, I was sent to Rotterdam to organize publicity for the 1,000th visitor to the Swedish exhibition. I had the press ready on a Saturday morning and a photographer was ready to shoot the lucky visitor. I told the photographer, that we were not counting anymore to look for the 1,000th visitor. "Now we are looking for a young and attractive girl, a real looker, who would get attention in the paper", I told him. Now I had box of Swedish cutlery, a bouquet of flowers, which I had bought at the flower stall across from the building and I was prepared for the presentation. Then it happened. A beautiful girl, just the one I described to the photographer came in with an older lady, obviously her mother. Now I had to stall them, while another box of cutlery and another bouquet of flowers were being brought in. I talked about the exhibition and tried to explain about Swedish products, then we gave them the bouquets and the boxes of cutlery, but the two looked so puzzled, somehow. Then they asked: "You mean to say that this is not the art embroidery exhibition?" "No, sorry madam, that exhibition is upstairs, but may I show you this exhibition before I bring you upstairs?" I was relieved, that they did not object.

Times had changed in Canada and we were anxious to try again. Now, on our return, we would have a chance to get work, and could look after Brian's needs, because of Medicare. He was in need of knee braces now, and soon after our return, we took care of that. Life had turned around and we entered a memorable period in our lives. A dark period was behind us and Lydie was a tower of strength. We did everything together, while in Holland, and we would continue to do so in the days, weeks and years ahead.

CHAPTER FOURTEEN

FRESH START

The MacLean Hunter, the Canadian publisher of English and French magazines was seeking people and I was hired soon after my arrival back into the city, we wondered how we would manage with the kids, but we did, and we prospered. My job was proofreading both English and French magazine galley proofs and I was unionized and my wages were a bit of the envy of the journalists, yet I made many friends among them and this time it was our social life that had improved so much. My father's interest in medals was one of the many things I inherited from him and when I met a sculptor who was one of the very artists in Canada sculpting medals in clay to be cast in bronze, we seemed to have something in common. She was sculptor, Hungarian born, Dora de Pedery-Hunt, Canada's famous medal sculptor, who had worked a great deal with the Mint in Ottawa and through her, I met another Hungarian, Stephen Mezei and his wife Rosza. He was a writer and a highly cultured person and while he was Jewish, his wife, also a Hungarian was Roman Catholic and a painter.

Stephen started a Writers and Artists club, which he named the Family Compact and he introduced me to a number of its members and then invited me to join them. This was real fun for me, but a few years later I wondered about the fact, that most members were famous, except me! There was Ian Tyson and his German girlfriend Sylvia. They became a famous duo and produced a great number of records. He was singing and played guitar and she was singing as well. An abstract painter by the name of Martel, who sometimes was trying to sell his paintings door-to-door and a journalist, George Jonas, also a Hungarian, who was specializing in being controversial. May be it was to attract attention at the time and he was well known in theatre circles. Then we had John Robert Colombo, who collected anecdotes and quotations by well known Canadian personalities. He had drawers full, all written on little cards and I asked him what we was going to do with all that material and then he told me, that he was going to collect them in books to be published. He did just that and many of his books are still available in the public libraries. He became not only very successful, but also popular.

The last member was Peter Gzowsky, who was a journalist and later a broadcaster. He was a descendent of a famous Canadian engineer of Polish descent. He worked for the same company as I did, but in another capacity. Stephen Mezei opened a small gallery for small sculptures and medals and called it the Minotaur gallery and Dora de Pedery-Hunt made a medal depicting this legendary beast one side of the medal and she had it cast in several copies, of which I still have one. He also published a satirical magazine named PINCH and I did the layout for him. He also lectured part time at the university and wrote books. I remember him fondly.

Sometimes, in life we meet people and after becoming friends, we find out that we have a family connection. In Toronto, I met Henning von Bredow, who was working with the Canadian Broadcasting Corporation, and was a sound engineer at symphony concerts being broadcast on Radio. I wrote my father about our new friend and his wife Jane, who grew up on Prince Edward Island. My father wrote back to inform me that the family von Bredow was living in Germany a couple of hundreds years ago across from our family. Our family was very well off, while his family was going through a very difficult period. To help that family out, our family bought their very large home. It is very well possible that there is much more to this story, but for us it was just something that happened years ago, but it was a coincidence just the same, one of a number of which we cannot possibly explain.

Now we were in the position to buy a bungalow in Downsview and we were looking at one near the airport behind the backyard, which had a high hedge. I wanted to see what was behind that hedge, and then I noticed that a runway ended just behind it. . "Do you know that a runway ends behind that hedge?", I asked the real estate agent, "Yes, but that runway is not in use anymore" and only moments later a large De Haviland airplane flew very low over the hedge and over the house. We looked at the agent, who knew, that there was not to be any sale this time.

The hospital for Sick Children and Sunnyview Hospital helped us with therapy for Brian and braces and crutches were made to order. We took Alan and Brian swimming three times a week and in spite of his handicap, Brian became a good swimmer. When Brian was ten years old, we lived in our own home in Willowdale and he was still swimming, now in a therapeutic pool in town. Eight adults were also in the pool and Brian had been swimming for four years and was working on his third level of the Red Cross handicapped program. He was doing well in school and every morning a big burly taxi driver put his wheelchair in the trunk of his car, carefully, not to touch the radio.

Then in August 1961, Glenn was born. The closest hospital, one built by a religious organization, did not serve meat or coffee, which was a real sacrifice for the new mother, but she endured this hardship in the knowledge that she soon would be able to catch up. When I came in to take mother and son home, I was told by a doctor, that the baby had to stay for another night. "You can pick him up tomorrow morning, because this afternoon he will be circumcised" We told the doctor that we would not allow an operation on a healthy baby and I took the mother and the baby home. Seven months later, we took him to the Hospital for Sick Children, because he had many bruises and a swollen spleen. At first they thought of child abuse, but soon apologized and they told us that the baby had hemophilia. We were thinking of the doctor in the Seventh Day Adventist hospital, where he was born and we thanked our lucky stars that he was not circumcised. "What do we do now, doctor?" Then he answered: "You live with the child for six months and you have all the answers, so don't ask me". Once a week from now on we took him to the hospital for an infusion of plasma, a process that took time. Brian went to physiotherapy and Alan went to school. Since Brian went to a special school, we had our hands full.

Yet, we had an interesting time in Ontario. We traveled through the province and even did some mountain climbing with Brian on my shoulders and often we did some tent camping. Everything we did included the three boys. One day we were traveling on the highway and came near Barrie, when we decided to have supper in a new Highway restaurant, just outside the town. Entering the restaurant, we chose a round table in the middle of the room. We asked for a high chair for Glenn. They brought us menu cards and then we ordered. Meanwhile, Glenn was playing with a penny and all of a sudden, we asked each other: "where is that penny, he was playing with?" "He did not swallow it, did he?" That concerned us, because, being a hemophiliac, we did not know how it would affect his throat so early in the game. With visions of a bleeding throat, we cancelled the lunch, grabbed the kids and drove to the hospital in Barrie. On our arrival, we went into emergency and after much waiting, had our turn. Eventually a doctor had a look at him and said "Nothing to worry about. Look in his diaper tomorrow, and you'll find a bright shiny penny". Now we would return to the restaurant, but the exit was very crowded as two ambulances had arrived and they were unloading.

We passed the cars with the flashing lights asking around what had happened. "An accident at the new restaurant on the highway", was the answer. Now we were anxious to find out and we returned to the restaurant and on our return, we were in shock. The front window was blown out. Fire trucks and police cruisers and ambulances were in front of the building. We left the car, walked over and looked in. Our table was gone and in its place was a big hole and we could look straight into the basement. A doctor, his wife and three children were sitting around our table, when the boiler beneath them blew up. The doctor was killed, his wife seriously wounded and so were the three kids. We did not have a late lunch after all, because we had lost our appetite. And we realized, a mere penny saved us.

In the fall, Lydie's father died and that was a real blow to her. She loved him dearly and now her mother was left alone. She was to pay us a visit many months later and, while in Toronto, the medical profession was anxious to find out if in her family in the past members had hemophilia, as it is brought in through the mother's side of the family. One day, Glenn found a fishing rod in the basement and he put it in his mouth while pushing it along the floor pretending it was a trumpet. When the other end hit a wall, it went into his throat and bleeding started profusely. We took him immediately to the hospital to get massive doses of plasma, which stopped the bleeding. He had been in the hospital twice while unconscious. Before he left the hospital, the doctor asked him how he coped with his problem and he answered: "I can't do things the other kids can. It kind of bugs me. I would like to climb trees and play hockey" . Going to the hospital did not bother Glenn at all. "After a while, you get used to it. I don't mind the needle at all, but when my knees start swelling, I have an awful lot of pain." Although he was always cheerful, he wished he could ride a bike.

When Lydie started working as a social worker in Willowdale, we bought a house there and moved. Meanwhile at my job at MacLean-Hunter one day, an editor of an English version of a trucking magazine entered my office. He had a galley proof in his hand, signed by me and yet he asked me: "did you do that?" and I pointed at my signature. "How dare you to change my editorial." He was standing there, shirt sleeves rolled up showing an anchor tattoo. "I had my education in the U.K and a foreigner, whose first language is not even English has the gall to rewrite my editorial." Now he was foaming under his moustache and around his mouth. How would I answer this man? His writing and grammar was terrible and he did not have any idea about style. I could not let this go to print, and felt, that if I changed it, I would do him a favour, although I did know that I was not hired to do this. Then I answered: "Don't you think, it runs better this way?" He then turned around and walked out.

CHAPTER FIFTEEN

FLASHBACK

Born in The Hague, Lydie's parents moved to Voorburg, when she was probably between 1 and 2 years old. Her brother Ger was 5 years older and the difference in ages was the cause, the same situation happened as in my family with my older brother and sister. When she started public school, Ger went to high school and each of them had their own friends. They had very caring parents, full of love and what she remembers from her youth, that she had lots of fun, which is a joy for her to remember. Then in 1940 came the war with all the problems it brought. The first two years were not so bad; there was lots of food to eat and enough coal in the stove to keep warm in the winter. However, the Germans stole more food and other things people needed, to keep alive and she remembers vividly, that her mother walked with her to a small farmers' village with a pair of her father's boots to exchange for a bag of oats. She also remembers walking with her bike around the street to hide it, while the Germans were at the other end of the street were going from house to house, stealing bikes. And the endless search for anything to eat and or burn in the tiny little stove they used to cook on.

During the later part of 1944 her brother was picked up and sent to Germany, where he promptly escaped and fled back to Holland, were, after a long voyage by train, he arrived. A good Dutchman helped him over the border and into the country where he found an address in Borger, in the Province of Drenthe, and where he hid himself. In the meantime, in December Lydie said good bye to her parents as she had an address in the province of Groningen, where they still had enough to eat, while in the western part of the country, everyone was without food. This way, her parents still had a ration card for four people, while they were only with the two of them, a way of keeping alive. She went with a open truck from the Red Cross and with other young people to Groningen and when she crossed the so-called Yssel Line, a bridge in the east, people were standing on the road, dealing out loaves of bread, which they literally devoured. Dropped off somewhere in the city of Groningen, she had to ask her way to the village of Borger, where she was received with open arms. She still remembers the people there and at the evening meal, where they were all sitting around the table. In the kitchen and on the table was a very large pot with hunks of lamb and inches of fat floating in the pan. That night she was sick as a dog, because her stomach was unable to handle the food, after such a long time without any food it all.

What happened in the following weeks, she never understood. The same people, who received her so nicely, sent her to a butcher in the village, because they did not want to keep her any longer. During that time she came into the possession of her brother's address and decided to walk to where he was staying. After a long walk of which she remembered little else than jumping into the woods, when planes came overhead, she arrived there and found her brother. However she could not stay there and somehow, these people were he was staying knew a very small farm with one pig and some acreage where she could stay. These people, poor as they were, were people with hearts of gold. She became a member of this small family and stayed with them until she could return home, which was several months later. There she saw the end of the war, freed by Canadian and Polish troops. The farmers in the neighbourhood had built a shelter, where they all hid during the fighting. At the end of the fighting, a German soldier came into her shelter with a big gun in his hands. He asked to stay and showed them pictures of his family in Baiern in Southern Germany. They did not want them, but they were afraid, that he would shoot them all. Lydie told him to give her the gun, which he did and then they told him to get out and give himself up to the Canadians. She never found out whatever may have happened after that.

In August, at last, she hitchhiked home with some other young people and arrived safely. Nobody knew she was coming home as nobody had a telephone yet and no mail delivery. She remembers that her mother was looking out of the window and all at once, she saw her walking up the road. She stormed out of the house, but instead of going to her, she disappeared around the corner of the house, reappearing a few minutes later with her dad in tow. He was on his wooden shoes and had a rake in his hands. He had been working in his little veggie garden in a plot of land around the corner. Well, they had a big celebration and all four members of the family were together again. Her brother came home earlier as he was able to get a pass, acting as a labourer. That was needed to start building up the devastation especially in the western part of the country. After several months, she went back to school, having lost a year of schooling. She finished her studies in social work during the following years, when her brother, who had married and settled with wife and baby in Canada, who sent a letter to the family, telling them, that his wife had left him and that he needed someone to look after the baby. In the years following, Lydie showed a lot of tenacity, which came in handy, because her life was going to be eventful as well.

CHAPTER SIXTEEN

THE PHOTOGRAPHER AND THE PAINTERS

After supper, photographer Chits in The Hague called his son. "We have to go back to the studio to finish that job. You have to get used to the idea that many times, we have to work nights and even on Saturdays". "Look at this glass negative'" he said, back in the studio. "This is an example of my best work". His son knew that he still had a lot to learn, although, now as a partner, he did not want to be reminded of that fact. "But look what you had to work with", he offered. It was true, young Mr. van der Kolk was a very handsome young bridegroom and together they made a very handsome couple. Later, the print showed two people, just married. The bride was wearing a long chiffon dress with ribbons falling down from the waist and there, very elegantly, a corsage of white flowers. The young girl had a high collar and smiled proudly, her arm in his, while his new husband, in dark wedding costume, holding a top hat, his mustache neatly trimmed, looked young and confident. The photographer only knew the girl. He had heard, that her grandfather was a foundling, found in a basket. The family name, Lak, came from the discovery, of embroidered initials on the little sheet L.A.K. and above the initials a small crown.

He had never met young van der Kolk. The girl told him that he came from Zwolle or thereabouts. His family had owned a large island near Kampen, and most of the family lived there in the area. After making all the prints, he was about to close his studio, when he noticed the calendar. Tomorrow is the first of March, he thought, while he ripped a page from the calendar. "Time flies", he thought, looking at yesterday's date: 29th of

February 1896. Why would anybody marry in the winter?

Lydie did not know her grandparents on her mother's side, but she had heard that her grandfather rescued many people from drowning in Rotterdam harbour. He was known to be a snappy dresser. The parents of Jan lived in Voorschoten, a town nearby and when Lydie was little, she played with "Spits", a large Shepard dog, large enough to ride on. Her mother was a direct descendant of a famous painters family of which Herman van der Mijn was the head. He was born in Amsterdam in 1684 and until his death in 1741, he was a very busy man. His teacher Edward Stuver, was only interested in painting fruits and flowers, but he was more interested in painting historical scenes and even portraits. His fame spread all over Europe, first at the Royal House of Prussia, where he painted for the von der Pfalz family, then to Holland and again to Paris. There he tried to sell some of his paintings to the Duke of Orleans, but his prices were too steep. Later, he left for London, and there he lived many years. His portraits fetched large sums of money, and some were large, life size. The Duke of Chandos shelled out 500 pounds sterling, a real princely sum in those days. Then he painted the Prince of Wales, and this portait was such a success, that a sister of the Duke of Chandos, who was an artist in her own right, asked this Dutch artist, if she might paint a portrait of him.

When asked to restore the paintings in the Royal palace in Burleight, he asked 500 pounds sterling and he indeed received this sum, which was unusually high. Herman van der Mijn had one fault, however. He spent his money as fast as it came in. In 1736, he was deeply in debt, and it seemed that everybody in London were after his money. One day he packed up and left London. He actually fled to return to Holland. This was a good move, because almost immediately the Prince of Orange offered him a stipend of 1500 guilders per year. Five years later, the artist left once again for London, thinking, that now he could do even better, but it was not to be. He died there after one year, surrounded by his family, who would find out very soon that he did not have one-pound sterling to his name.

Little is known with regard to his wife, but his children made names for themselves as accomplished painters. The oldest, Gerhard, was born before his father left for London. He was born in 1706 in Amsterdam. Like his father, he mostly painted portraits and historical paintings. He too worked later in life in London. His sister Cornelia, born in Amsterdam in 1717, also painted portraits, but was also an accomplished flower painter, and when she moved to London, to follow her father, she had such a success, that she received many commissions. Her three years older brother Francis was a copper engraver, but he painted as well. He was born in 1719 in Amsterdam and another brother, Robert who was born in London in 1724, like Francis, learned the trade from his father. But it was George, however, who, of all the children is still the most famous of the six children. George was born in London in 1723 and still very young. He was the most interested in his father's trade. The family still had many connections with Amsterdam and, bent on adventure, George left for Amsterdam before his twenty-first birthday. He only reached 39 years of age and because of that, he was less prolific than his family members, but his talent was well known in this city, where over the years many Dutch masters worked and lived. The descendants of Herman van der Mijn, when visiting the major museums of Europe, point at the work of the master and say to their children: "He was our forefather, you know!"

CHAPTER SEVENTEEN

MOVE TO THE SEA

It was the year that we became Canadians. The whole family was present, when Secretary of State, The Hon. Judy LaMarsh handed us our citizenship certificates. It was early in 1968 and the beginning of a full year of events. On a beautiful morning in the spring, we decided to pack a lunch and go to a Provincial Park North of Toronto. The sun was already getting warm and the children wanted to go right after breakfast. When we arrived, we found a line up of at least a thousand cars. The park opened at ten o'clock and the park swallowed all the cars with ease, but this was the topic of the day. Do we want crowds for our kids to grow up in or would the kids be better off living in a country setting, where they could have pets and where the pressures of city life would be absent? We knew that buying a house in Ontario would be impossible as even far away from the city, the prices would not be within our means. We decided to look elsewhere. What about another province?, we wondered. We talked it over with the kids, we told them, that, since they had three voices and we only two, their decision would have a great influence on deciding where we would will be headed. First we talked about all kinds of provinces, and we eliminated many for different reasons. Then we were thinking of the Maritimes because of our past, which was filled with beaches and the sea. We decided to rent movies and books from the Library and then the choice fell on the Province of New Brunswick.

Lydie took four days off from her job, flew to Fredericton and rented a car. She made a lot of pictures for the family at home, talked to potential employers, did the same in Saint John and then drove to Hampton. After her visit, she flew back and told us that Fredericton was the seat of the provincial government and was also a university town. If you're not a member of either institution, you would have a hard time settling in. Saint John was different, she found the people very friendly and she felt welcome there. There was a need for a seasoned social worker and everything looked good. Then she drove to Hampton to get a feel for the country and after returning, she suggested that we look for a place halfway Saint John and Hampton, in the beautiful valley there. This good news prompted us to sell the house and right after the last school day, Lydie, Brian and Glenn flew to Saint John. Alan and I packed the old green Ambassador station wagon with what the movers had left behind and we drove with the cat in a box to Quebec to a town with the funny name St. Louis du Ha Ha. We stopped for supper and rented a room in a motel. While we were watching television, we heard screeching in the box and when we looked in, the cat had given birth to three kittens, but none were alive. Now we slipped outside to find a spot to bury the kittens.

When we arrived in Saint John, it was late in the evening and near a large building in a park like setting, we stopped to look at our map. Immediately a police cruiser stood behind us and an officer told us that we're not allowed to stop there. "Where are you heading? "For the Wandlyn Motel" "That's too difficult to explain'" he said "Just follow me". At midnight we arrived at the hotel and took a room upstairs. In the morning we called our family. "Where are you?", they asked, "Right across the hall", we said. Then I looked out of the window and saw a big furniture warehouse with a name sign at the front. "There is our furniture", I said to Alan.

We decided to pitch a tent in Rockwood Park, which is a large city park, and from there we were going house hunting. The boys' thought this was a great idea. We had a flat wagon, and we took turns, pulling this all through the park, and Brian, the passenger, thought this was cool. We put the kids into the station wagon drove to Hammond River, the area identified by Lydie as the most desirable and found a two story house on a acre of sloping land, at the bottom of which was a creek. It had a septic tank, a party-line phone and a well and while we were not familiar with these unusual elements, we thought we could live with that. I asked the real estate agent, who was an elderly man, about the property taxes. "50 dollars", he answered. "Fifty dollars a month for a well and a septic tank? I don't think so" "If I ask that question in Toronto, I get the same answer, because they don't like the idea of quoting, what the yearly charge is. "I did not quote a charge per month, but per year", the agent added. Four days later he phoned us to tell us that another prospect offered $4,000 more, because, further up the road, they had decided, that they did not like strangers moving into the area. Since the deal was closed, they just had to put up with us, we thought.

Lydie started her job as a social worker, and I was offered a job with the telephone company's public relations department, a job I loved, writing and publishing the company magazine, writing press releases, organizing the dedication of new buildings in the province, write and design booklets and many other interesting chores. The kids started school in a one room schoolhouse in nearby Nauwegiwauk and Alan was allowed there to start the potbellied stove and I could not help remembering my army days in Ede, where we used the planks out of our beds to get warm. The teacher taught three classes at the same time, but that would last only one year as the school would be torn down, and the students would go with a yellow school bus to Hampton. Forty years later, Alan, now a real estate appraiser, had to appraise a house next to the spot were the schoolhouse was located. And when he was measuring the outside of the house, a woman came out of the door to look, what he was doing. Then she had a good look at him and with an outstretched arm she pointed with her finger at him and said; "You were the boy, who broke my basement window!". Perhaps he was playing ball forty years ago, when he was a student next door.

The house used to be a farmhouse, just like the one next door, where old John Gilliland lived alone with his cats. The road ended at the farm of Joe Steele. The old homestead was all that was left from an old farm. Across the road were some cottages on the river. Sometimes the water was so low, that the cows from the Steele farm waded through the river and made a beeline for the acre of lush grassland on the other side and behind our house, which had yet to be cut. When that happened, we were chasing the cows back to the other side of the road. We felt like cowpokes.

That scene excited the boys; they were still city slickers, but liked their fun. Late at night, Glenn was crying and Lydie said: "Here we go again". She rushed upstairs. He had another bleeding episode, probably his knees again. We knew that only massive doses of plasma would stop the bleeding and we helped him dress quickly. For an eight year old, he had seen the inside of a hospital too often. We went to the car, carrying him and found that someone had let the air out of our tires. Someone on the road did not like people from Upper Canada, which we knew then, that they meant Ontario. We tried to call the RCMP, but someone else was on the party line. We asked the person, to please get off the line as we had to take our son to the hospital. "A likely story" the woman said and did not hang up. We went to our neighbour across the road, a kind elderly man, who brought us to the hospital. He was on the verge of going to bed. The next day we called the telephone company and the woman was cut off for good.

Word from Holland was not good either. Ies, my mother, was in hospital and my father was alone by himself in their apartment, and he sensed, that she would never come home again. She was his constant companion for fifty years and the years had been good, in spite of all the problems, during the war, and the anxieties about the children. In March, she died quietly and my father felt a great loss. She had been a wonderful partner and mother and he was grateful for the many years, he had lived with her. A month after the funeral, Jaap was offered a free ticket with the KLM, the Dutch airline. It was the inaugural flight to Montreal and he took the opportunity to visit us for three days. On his return, he gave my father a ticket to Canada to give him a chance to visit us in August for a month too. When he came, he helped us to build an open garage. He loved to walk up the road and from that vantage point, he marveled at the river in the valley at the other side of the highway, where he sat in the grass. He adored the children and to listened Alan talk about his flying lessons with the Air cadets, then watched the other two playing with their dogs, cats and rabbits.

Since I had taken an electric lawnmower with me from Toronto, I started to mow the grass using three extension cords. The Italian lady next door, wife of a barber, who had a shop in town, looked at me from her front window and I saw her shaking her head. My father watched old Mr. Rushton across the road, wearing his hip waders, standing in the river trying to catch a salmon for supper. When it was lunchtime, Betty, his wife, opened the kitchen window, and called him to lunch by blowing on her Boy Scout whistle, which hung on a string around her neck. But what he enjoyed the most was the Nauwegiwauk Country Fair, listening to the fiddlers. He was a trained musician, playing the violin well, but this fiddle music, he had never heard and was fascinated by it. After the death of his beloved Ies, this holiday was for him the best medicine, he could ever get.

Brian had a problem at school. The school did not have a wheelchair ramp and when we made a presentation to the school board, one member said: "My daughter is deaf, and she does not get special treatment, so why should you". Then we asked the only hematologist in the province at the time, to make needles, concentrate, which was then used in stead of plasma, and other supplies available, so that we could help our son ourselves at home and he could help himself later on. "No way" was the answer. "As a matter of fact, you should seriously think of keeping him in the hospital until he is eighteen." "No way" we answered. We told him it was done in Ontario and was normal practice. It was also welcomed by the hospitals, where they had a personnel shortage. We asked Glenn's former doctor in Toronto, to write our hematologist a strong worded letter, what he did. Now the hematologist changed his mind, and started bragging that he was so progressive, that he would start this program all over the province. Now we did not have to go out in the middle of the night, to go to the hospital anymore.

The old green Ramble Ambassador station wagon, which we brought from Ontario, gave us problems. We needed a new carburetor. A new one would cost $150, because it was a four barrel one. Lydie decided to buy a kit instead, took the carburetor off the engine block, spread a newspaper out on the kitchen table and went to work. "What you are doing?" I asked her, "Do you know what to do?" "No I don't, but if I find a spring in the envelope, I look for the same one in the carburetor and switch them". It seemed logical enough. After putting all the parts into our carburetor, she placed it back on the engine block and the engine purred like a kitten again. The car worked well and after six months we sold it to an office cleaner. Then for weeks after the sale, we saw the car stalled on the bridge, on a plaza, all over town. You could not miss it. The electric rear window was still half open, as it was stuck for a year now, a mop handle was sticking out and after a while, we never saw our green station wagon again.

Glenn's knees were bothering him a great deal, and we bought a brace for support. One Sunday morning the boys asked me to bring them to the Peninsula across the Kennebecasis River and we took the ferry and then drove to a farm. We were instructed to stay in the car. "What are you guys up to anyway?" we wanted to know. But the answer was simple. "You'll see..." Then after ten minutes, while we were waiting in the car at the beginning of the driveway, they returned, carrying two burlap bags. They placed these on the back seat and we drove back to the ferry. While crossing the river, someone was pulling my hair. "Cut it out, you guys", I said and they started laughing, then I turned my head and now I was looking into the face of a lamb. They had bought two of them. "Now I know what you are up to, but have you any idea what is involved raising sheep?" "You don't have a pen, where do you think you would put these animals?" The answer was very easy and they had it all figured out. "Oh, for the time being we'll put them in the front porch and we get some straw from Mr. Gilliland next door". They already had a name for one of them; they called him, Lambchops. As it turned out, Lambchops had a mind of his own. He stepped on our ducks and rabbits and chased the ducklings, but both of the lambs grew up fast, while they helped me by eating the grass of our acre. I bought the heaviest chains, I could find to tether these animals, but they were getting so strong that they broke the shackles in no time. In the fall, a man was at the door, and a heavy three-ton truck was standing in the driveway, while I was watching inside from the window. The three boys were outside next to the truck and I saw the man hauling a thick and large wallet on a chain, out of his back pocket. Now money changed hands and then they lifted the sheep into the truck, and the man drove off. "Oh, that was their scheme all along", I thought, they were not pets at all, they were a business!"

CITY SLICKERS IN THE COUNTRY

"Where you're from?" our new neighbour asked us. "Tranna", I said, and he immediately knew that I was from the City of Toronto. "You better change your license plate right away, because otherwise they would not accept you being an Upper Canadian". "Upper, what?" I asked. I wondered what kind of people lived in Hammond River, or was it Nauwegiwauk?". "Confusing", we thought. Ours was a two-story farmhouse with an acre of grass at the back, sloping down to a little creek. On one side there was a farm and the other side an apartment building. The owner, Gerry DeFaszio had a barbershop in the City. We settled in nicely with our three sons and now we decided to get a doctor. The nearby Village of Hampton had three of them and when we picked one of them, we phoned Dr. Robb's office; that's what we thought. The woman at the other end of the phone answered with "County Jail". Obviously I had the wrong number, but before we had a chance to hang up, she asked, if we were looking for Dr. Robb. And so it was, she was obviously moonlighting.

Doug Robb was not only a very talented physician, but became a friend of the family. On Sunday, January 1st one year, the doorbell rang and while we were still in our pajamas, Doug Rob was standing on the doorstep with a block of wood in his hands and a box of shortbread. "An old Scottish tradition", he explained, "On New Year's Day, you visit your best friends first and bring them wood to wish them a warm hearth and bread to wish them a full stomach." We made breakfast for him and afterwards he told us that he had to leave, because he was worried about a patient. He stepped into his Morris Minor and we yelled at him: "Don't you ever take a day off?" But he waved at us, his arm out of the window. One day he phoned us and invited us Friday afternoon to have a glass of wine with him. We went to his house, but his wife, Isabel, told us that he was still on the road, but she invited us in to wait for him in front of the fireplace. Then he came in the room. Dropped his leather "toolkit" on the floor and sat down with us. Then the telephone rang and he went up to take the call after which he excused himself, because he had to see a patient. "You are exhausted and in no condition to drive a car, we'll bring you there." and he gratefully accepted. I drove him to a house on the other side of the highway and he asked me to wait for him. He walked to the house and entered. This house was completely dark. I saw the light going on downstairs, then one upstairs and after a while these lights went out, and he appeared again in the doorway. "What happened?" I asked, as he was laughing so hard. Then he said, "I had trouble finding the light switches. But when I put the light on, I saw that the son was sleeping on the couch and obviously drunk."

"Then I went upstairs to look for the woman and when I found her in one of the bedrooms, I asked her if this was the bed she planned to sleep in and after the needle, she would be out cold, and I prepared the needle and with the needle in my hand I was going to sit at the edge of the bed and when I sat down, the bed collapsed. I gave her the needle, tucked her in and went downstairs again." One day, I asked a neighbour if there was a dentist around or in Hampton and he answered with: "Not exactly". This was a strange answer and an explanation would be a big help. He explained, that Dr. Snow could, and even would, pull a tooth or molar, but he didn't have a license to give you any Novocaine for the pain, but everybody in town knew that in one of the drawers of his desk, he had a bottle of the best and a shot glass, and so now going to a pretend dentist was not a bad idea.

Winter in Hammond River meant snow and between our house and that of farmer Steele at the end of the road, lived a woman, who loved her large and noisy snow mobile and she loved to race over the road with the help of a little liquid courage. One day she somehow managed to steer this monster between our house and Gerry's building and raced down our sloping acre. Realizing that the creek was the end of the line, she managed to turn around and raced up the hill towards our house, but since Gerry's house was on higher land, she hit the side of the driveway, lost control over her monster and flew into our front porch, without even touching the sides of the door opening. Taking that heavy snowmobile out of the front porch was a real challenge.

CHAPTER NINETEEN

MARITIMERS

We both needed to drive cars for our work. I had my little blue company car, and Lydie drove her own car to her clients. In 1962, Lydie had an accident. An elderly couple hit her car at an intersection due to a tree branch was that was hiding a stop sign. Nine years later she had surgery on a slipped disc, a leftover from that mishap.

It was a sunny summer morning, when I arrived at the airport of Saint John. I was planning to fly to Bathurst for my work, because I did not have the time to pick up the company car. A new airline was just established there and the owner was standing in the open doorway to prepare for the inaugural flight. Looking out on the tarmac waiting for the plane to arrive. "I heard that your airplane is painted pink" I said, "funny colour", I added. "Why don't you paint your whole fleet another colour, like blue". I asked, knowing very well, that he had only one plane, but thought, that the word "fleet" would sound more impressive. "We can't afford that", he replied, "if we do that, we have to take out two seats, paint weighs a lot, you know. The alternative would be to scrape off al the old paint and that would cost a bundle. We bought the plane from a cosmetics firm", he volunteered, thinking that his very first customer would find that interesting. "Oh, there's my plane. She's a bit late, because the pilot had a test run with an officer of the Department of Transport. He has not his New Brunswick license yet". Now he was looking at me and realized that he had talked too much. "Don't worry, he's a seasoned pilot, he was flying for a large corporation in New England for years". The plane landed and the two pilots walked towards the Terminal building.

The owner, not thinking about me, ran up to the two men and asked anxiously "Did you pass?" Then he turned around to see if I was still standing in the door way. The Department of Transport officer turned to the pilot and I heard him asking. "Would you like me to go with you to Bathurst? You don't seem to be too familiar with this model" and he laughed and added, "I can show you the ropes". The owner, realizing what was happening, tried to interrupt the conversation. He was now in a panic, because, since I was now within earshot, I might cancel the flight. No wonder the plane had already received a nickname. They called it the Pink Panther. Pink Panther indeed, I thought, it does not look like an airline to me. In the same year, the Pink Panther had an accident, causing permanently grounding of the "fleet" It effectively killed the airline.

We met many Maritimers, a number of which came from other countries, like us, but some were people you would never forget. One of those was John Copeland. It's hard to remember when we first met him, whenever that was, but we became friends almost instantly. He liked art and was an accomplished painter, but like me, strictly an amateur. It was a hobby. He was well educated, at the University of Cambridge, no less, and he was a teacher with a specialty, teaching children with special needs. Since I had an interest in children with physical handicaps, we hit it off very fast. When John saw an ad in a Canadian Educational magazine, which he read in England, he saw that in Saint John they had a need for someone of his caliber, and the school superintendent soon understood fully, that he had made a very good decision. John came to Canada with his wife and settled in his new country. Unfortunately, the marriage ended, because his wife could not handle the change, and was homesick. John, now alone, moved to a small apartment, which became his home in Fairvale near Saint John, not far from his school. Looking outside at the garden below, with the flowering trees, it soon became his home and his life gradually became interesting, filled with teaching, preaching and painting.

While he was brought up a Catholic, he lost interest and made friends with a Protestant minister, who asked him to conduct services in a number of small churches, in a nearby Peninsula, and in the country. On a Sunday, he went to one, was picked up for lunch and brought to another. It probably was a bit more of a social thing, because he loved to be with people all the time. He walked to school a lot, no matter what the weather. He went out, wearing boots, his black suit and white shirt, with his Cambridge tie or on occasion his RAF tie and walked to school. In the summer, he met on his way a woman with a pram. "Hello Mr. Copeland, do you remember me? I was in your class". The new mother had seen him from afar, because of his white head of hair.

He had two daughters, who decided to stay in England to get their teaching degrees, but over time, he lost track of them. Besides, they felt, that he had abandoned them, going to far away Canada with their mother. Now he longed for them, but he realized, that they might not even want to hear about him. He asked us what he should do. We suggested to him to get in touch with the Salvation Army, which had a department looking for lost relatives all over the world. They did find them but told him, that they still needed permission from them to reveal their whereabouts. Eventually, they came over to pay him a visit. When he retired, the teachers threw a party for him and that included a stretched limousine, picking him up and bringing him to school. With the roof wide open, he was standing up, sticking out of the roof, waiving and smiling ear-to-ear, waiving to the children. He loved 'his' children and often, when a child fell and was hurt, he took it on his lap, and they looked on him as a kind grandfather. The day after his retirement, he put his boots on and walked to school. "What are you doing here, John, you are retired now". He could not get to the idea easily. He often talked about the Royal Air Force. He longed to be a flyer, but that was not to be. Since he serviced the planes, the pilots admired his work, because they were aware that their lives were in his hands. He always waited for the pilots to come home from their long bombing raids into Germany, and when one did not came back he was distressed.

One day, we visited him and discovered that the electric kettle was plugged in, while obviously dry. Then we noticed that some food in the refrigerator was spoiled. Now we found out that he did not eat very well and we decided to arrange for Meals on Wheels, but when we came in again, the stack of pots was still standing there. He wondered what these were for, and since they were not his pots, he left it on the counter. While having a meal with us he seemed to have a healthy appetite, but had trouble knowing what to do with knife, fork and spoon. Eventually he wound up at an Alzheimer's unit of the hospital and later was able to get a room at a Veteran's hospital, where he was well cared for, but now everyone around him were total strangers, England was forgotten and he had no idea that he had daughters in England. When his life came to an end, we lost a good friend and we knew, that the many people, who crossed his path, where affected by his charm, his concern and his care. The children he taught are now the mothers of a new generation, still remembering with fondness a person, who made their difficult childhood a memorable period in their lives. He is certainly one person, we will never forget.

CHAPTER TWENTY

STONEYCROFT

When the boys were getting older, we decided to move to be closer to schools and shops and one Sunday morning we drove around the town of Quispamsis, not far away from where we had our farm house. We knew that we most likely had to build a wheelchair ramp and the house should have one floor and a basement. In a quiet street, we saw a man tacking a sign against a tree. We asked to have a look at the house. Lydie loved the fireplace and the cedar wood plank ceiling. The grounds around the house were full of construction debris, and rocks, a lot of rocks, and over time we would even find more rocks underground. This small subdivision was named after an original 1830's farmhouse at the entrance of a road that was actually a cul-de-sac. The road ended not far from the house, which had a play park right across the road. We loved the area and the valley is beautiful in all seasons. In summertime, the river is a blue ribbon and in the winter white and runs from the city along a string of villages. The village had a park on a cove in the river with a beach, nothing like Wassenaar, mind you. But it was still an attraction. A bit closer, a ferry brings people to the Kingston Peninsula and over the years more and more people moved there to be in the country, yet close enough to shops and other amenities. On Saturdays, families would take the ferry to go to two farmer's markets and have a real country breakfast. We started a garden, but we left all existing trees as we noticed that people cleared the gardens after they moved in and then grew grass all over. We were getting birds and other wild life, our neighbours never did. Over time, deer and raccoons were visiting and occasionally stole from the bird feeders.

We build a sunroom with large windows on the south side of the house, porches and a garage, which was left open in the front. We discovered something very strange. Our side of the road was always in the sun from early In the morning on and the sun circled our home, past our sunroom and in the afternoon we enjoyed the sun on the back of the house.

On our side of the road, the families were happy, stable and no serious problems were happening. On the other side, behind the playground in front of our house, all houses were in the shadow and only in the afternoon, they were getting the last rays of the sun. On that side, the families encountered death, divorces and all kinds of hardships and we often wondered if there was a connection with these situations and the lack of sunshine. It sounds a bit unbelievable, but the reality is there and that is why we were so happy to be on the sunny side of the street.

On sunny days, we walked over to a small lake, just steps away from the house, where a small beach, a park and benches made a perfect setting to watch the ducks and other waterfowl. The family was growing up and Brian went to the University, but after one year he thought that he was for us too much to handle. Alan had left the nest, and only Glenn was able to help us to get Brian in and out of bed, and the bathtub. He helped to dress him and then lifted him into his wheelchair. Since Glenn's knees were his weakest point, it was not an easy thing to do. Brian wrote a number of letters to special group homes where help would be available, one, called a Cheshire home, in Burlington, Ontario. It was a concept developed in England and seemed to be perfect for Brian. They could be independent, yet have all the needs they are looking for. Soon he would leave us. We offered to bring him, but he insisted to fly alone to Toronto, from where people from the home would pick him up with a wheelchair van. We brought him to the airport with a heavy heart. After some time Glenn joined him and then together they went job hunting. "We are a package deal" they insisted. Somehow they found an employer, who was so impressed with them, that after a period, they were given very responsible positions, with the result that they did very well. They rented an apartment together and, in spite of his problems, Glenn looked after his brother.

In the Cheshire home was also a wheelchair bound girl looking out of the window all day. Then Brian wheeled into the room and talked to her. "You have been sitting here every day. You don't work or go back to school. You pay less for your room and board than I, because I work for a living and you cash only your disability cheque. I give you one week to either get a job or go to school and if, after that week, you still look out of the window all day, I will see a board member I know, who will agree with me" The same week she applied to go to university to study library science and even before she finished her studies, she had obtained a permanent job in a nearby library. Alan stayed around, got married and became a father. Gradually, our lives were changing but we knew, we would never be bored, because it seems that somehow, we would get experiences, we could never even dream of and we wonder, what the next one would be in our checkered life.

CHAPTER TWENTY-ONE

VACATIONS

In the 1980's when our house was almost empty, and after 25 years together, the children were now independent from us. Thinking about that American captain after the war, who visited us from Paris and my nightly jeep ride with him, I wanted to smell that subway train again as it pushed the air out from the tunnel into the station. This time I did not sleep at an army base but in a real hotel and eat my croissants and drink my cafe-au-lait on a terrace overlooking the street. I wanted to visit Gensac again, where I worked with Spanish workers and danced in one of the bedrooms of the castle. Would I meet the two daughters of Monsieur Couraleau again?

We flew to London and took the ferry to Calais in France. We had a large orange suitcase, which we put in a luggage compartment near the door of the train. After a while, two men in uniform came onto the train. They each had a large dog with them and these dogs were sniffing on the suitcases. All of a sudden, one of the men asked, who the owners were of that orange suitcase and we identified ourselves. "Come with me" he said and we followed him. He asked us to open the suitcase, which we did, but they found nothing they were looking for. Perhaps our suitcase was standing near another one in the luggage compartment of the plane, one filled with drugs.

In Paris we found an inexpensive hotel and we stayed in Hotel du Danmark. We met a girl who was vacuuming the stairs and we discovered that she was from Winnipeg. She was Canadian student. Visiting Paris was great, and when we walked over to the Arc de Triumph, we wanted to see the eternal flame and the grave of the Unknown Soldier, but we found ourselves within a mass of people. Something was going on, yet we could not figure out what that was. On the rooftops of the buildings, in a circle around the monument, we saw people in black, all holding guns, ready to fire. We pushed through the crowd to have a better look, and then we arrived at scaffolding at the edge of the circle road around the Arc.

A man with a plastic tag on his lapel was directing the crowd near the scaffolding. Then a woman talked to him. "I am a German journalist, I have a press card, let me through", the woman shouted. Then the man in uniform said. "You have a red one, the new ones are green". Now the woman shouted obscenities at him. People were fighting to get onto the platform to get a better view. There was a man, with a large leather tube, almost a foot in diameter and at least three feet long. He was an American journalist. "Open that thing" the man said, thinking probably, that it contained a bazooka. He opened the tube and out came a large and wide camera lens unit. Then he took out his pocket a little camera and screwed that one onto the side of the "bazooka". "Can anyone lend me a shoulder?" he asked. But nobody took any notice of him. Now the crowds began to push in all directions and we crawled under the scaffolding.

Policemen were standing at the edge of the sidewalk all around the arc and one stood in front of us. I whistled at him and with my hands, I beckoned him to step aside a bit, so we would have a better view of whatever was to come. He complied, and then another man standing with us under the scaffolding told us was coming. "Breznev is going to lay a wreath under the Arc", he said. Then the traffic around the Arc started to thin out and then disappeared after which we saw four black Russian cars moving slowly around the Arc. They drove next to each other, but the front bumpers were not aligned, forming a long driving steel fence. Then they stopped. A small orchestra played the first verse of the Russian anthem, then one of the French one. The visitor stepped out of the car, was handed a wreath, which he placed near the flame. He stood in silence for a minute after he stepped into the car and now, slowly, the cars started to moved and left the scene and then the ever noisy traffic around the Arc de Triumph started to return. The crowds disbursed and the black figures with the guns on the rooftops disappeared. We returned to the Metro station to go back to the hotel, but when we arrived, ambulances were waiting with flashing lights and the entrance was cordoned off. Police were directing traffic and told people to move on. There had been a bomb blast and we walked on.

On top of a hill in Paris stands an imposing church, the Sacre Coeur (Sacred Heart) and we were planning to have a look. You go up the hill in a strange cable car because, while the seats are horizontal, the car itself has the same slant as the hill. This electric vehicle brought us to the top of the hill from where you have a great view of the city. After visiting the church with souvenir stands and priests, acting like carnival barkers, selling their wares, we returned and this time, we would take one of the two stairs down. After every so many steps is a flat area with benches to take a rest. About halfway we stopped, because we saw a couple doing strange things in the bushes, and at a closer look, we noticed that they were trapping pigeons. Why, we wondered, to make pigeon pie? Then, when the woman saw us looking, she ran up to us with a paper in her hands and said: "We have a license for that, do you want to check it?

We took the train to Bordeaux and took a bus to Gensac. We went to the town hall and learned, that the Couraleau family had moved away and that Monsieur Couraleau was not alive anymore. The daughters now lived in the Pyrenees somewhere. In the hall leading to the town office, we noticed pictures of local wine castles and then we saw a framed poster of New Brunswick, with a large photo taken somewhere in the province and underneath in large letters the name of the famed photographer: FREEMAN PATTERSON, who is a famous New Brunswick photographer. We asked were they found that poster, but they didn't know. In fact, they had never heard of New Brunswick or the photographer.

We went back to Libourne and the train station to travel more south and we stopped for the day in a town very close to the Spanish border with a beach on the coast. We noticed a very peculiar thing. The high and low tides were enormous, just as enormous as Southern New Brunswick, where we lived. We walked on the beach and all of a sudden the tide came in with a great force and we had to run for our lives. Then we had to climb a rock wall and we were forced to climb as fast as we could, which was very difficult, but in the nick of time, we made it to the top and we found ourselves at the rear of a children's home where we had to climb over a fence to get to a safe place.

With a Eurail pass, you have unlimited travel, ride first class and come and go as you wish. "Let's go to Italy", was the spur-of-the-moment plan and we went in a train going west. We wound up in Venice. We never made any reservations, because we could change plans in a minute. Venice is a great place to visit. We were both excited, but then, when we tried to get a room somewhere, we found that all hotels and bed and breakfasts were filled due to big conventions. We did not want to go out of town, because the way Venice is located, there was no out of town. You come into the city by train or car and the whole city is surrounded by water. When we walked through the city we saw on the sidewalk a boy selling souvenirs. He had displayed his giftware on a mat and he sat on a little stool. We asked, if he knew a place where we could stay. Then he rolled up his store and asked us to follow him, though little narrow streets on canals, they called Calle, then to a garden restaurant. He slipped in, went behind the bar and talked to the man behind the bar, who gave him keys. Again, he said in English, "Follow me" and then we arrived at a little canal street with mediaeval houses.

We read the nameplates on the door, and behind the names, we could understand that in this particular home, a doctor and a lawyer were living. Going through the front door, we were surprised to see, that the inside of these 16th century houses was very modern, with marble walls and stairs, which is a common building material in Italy. He opened an apartment door and we went in. It was not large, but very modern with all the conveniences. Then he asked us a dreadful question. "Please can I have your passports, I have to register you with the police. Don't worry, I will slip them under the door tomorrow morning". What are we to do? Canadian passports are very popular with criminal elements. Then we decided that he had us over a barrel and that we had no choice, but to take a chance. When we woke up in the morning, the first place we looked was at the door. And surely, the two passports were safely in front of the door.

After visiting this marvelous city, we traveled north again and stopped off in Milan for the night. We had our little game. When we arrived in a town or city, we would go out of the railroad station and take the road down and then the fourth street on the right again, there was a little local hotel, not meant for tourists, and often less expensive.

We counted the fourth street and lo and behold, we noticed a local hotel. We ordered a room, which was on the second floor, received a key hanging on a large piece of wood with a number on it and went to the elevator with our suitcase. This elevator had two half doors and it was a job to get the suitcase into the elevator, which caused us to get the giggles. We found our room upstairs and when we entered, we found a large four-poster bed. We dropped our suitcase on the floor and then jumped on our bed, which then collapsed and now we had to sleep on the floor. The next day we went to the station, but we were early for the train and we went into a park in front of the station, to sit on a bench to wait. Now two small barefooted children approached us. One was a girl with a large piece of cardboard under her arm and one was a boy who was holding up his hands.

The girl put the cardboard on our lap and now we understood their intentions, because her other hand was trying to grab our handbag. It didn't work and we chased them away. A little further along, there was a refreshment stand on wheels and when we looked up we saw a heavyset woman working on a coke machine with a gigantic screwdriver. The man, probably her husband, and a skinny one at that, was standing next to her and was watching with his hands on his side. Our Italian is just rusty at best, but never mind, Italians speak with their hands anyway and we were able to use ours to ask, using a few English and French words thrown in, why it was that his wife did all the work. He had an answer ready for us: He was the supervisor. This holiday was special, because we were free as a bird. Nothing was reserved, nothing was planned and we never knew, where we would lay our heads at night. But we had more fun, because every day was a surprise. When we returned, we were ready for the next episode, whatever life would bring.

Another memorable vacation was in Jamaica. The boys were drinking beer in a bar one day, discussing what to do about our upcoming anniversary. "Let's send them somewhere, but were?" one said, and after a discussion, they decided on Jamaica. What was interesting was the way they executed their plan. First they arranged with a travel agent that we would be going to Ocho Rios, and all would be prepaid. Then they told the agent that our destination would not be revealed until the last possible moment and if they told us, they would cancel the trip. "I can always find out, I know that travel agent", I said. And I did, but all she said was that we were going to Toronto, in other words, the scheme was working. First we flew to Toronto to visit Brian and Glenn in Burlington. I tried to find out, because I did not know what to pack, for a warm or a cold climate. But that did not work either. So, when we rang the door of the apartment in Burlington, the first question was "Where are we going?" they still stalled.

First a glass of wine, but eventually we knew it was Jamaica. In the Jamaican plane, which was bought from the defunct Freddy Laker Airline, everything was shaking terribly but the stewardess offered us champagne, knowing the reason from the carnations on our coats. When we did get out of the plane, a customs officer ran towards us, grabbed the carnations and ripped them off. "You are not allowed to import flowers", he said. This holiday was truly exceptional and on the last day, we returned our key to the desk, and they told us that we owed them a dollar for a telephone call. I wanted to give Canadian dollar but that was not accepted, then a Jamaican dollar and that was not accepted, they only wanted American dollars, which we did not have. "You cannot check out", the woman said. After talking to the manager, we were able to leave for the airport. When we arrived in Toronto, it was late and we missed the flight to Saint John, New Brunswick. In the morning we swam in the Gulf of Mexico and the temperature was a balmy 30 degrees, but in Toronto, it was also thirty degrees, but now below! All taxis were gone, so we checked our luggage in a locker, went out in the snow, and walked down the hill to a hotel, and in the morning they brought us back again. Sixty degrees difference in one day is too much. But we did have fun.

CHAPTER TWENTY-TWO

SECOND GENERATION

Raising three children, with two who have medical problems, is very difficult. While Lydie had a background in Social Work, we were ill prepared
to handle the situations. We just had to learn on the job, so to speak. We
also encountered little help initially, and we had to make choices. Some
of which were not very well thought out. When the children grew up,
however, we made at least one choice that was the right one. From an
early age, we taught the children to look after themselves. Some people
thought that this was a cruel thing to do, but, as it turned out, it helped
them greatly. As young as Glenn was at the time, we pushed an idea
that New Brunswick was regarded as irresponsible. We pushed the medical profession into letting Glenn give himself the weekly injections. He
learned how to cope with his limitations and that too turned out to be very
beneficial. Brian decided to move to Ontario, and that decision was made,
because we were not able to look after him any longer, as lifting him in
and out of bed, toilet or bathtub, became impossible. He arranged to live
in a Cheshire home, where he had all the facilities he needed to live an as
normal life as possible. They had strong personnel, doing all the lifting.

We made some bad mistakes, of course, and when the boys came up
with some of those as well, we said to them: "Don't do that, we did that
ourselves and it turned out badly". They heeded our advice, but made
other mistakes, that were bad too. Life is a learning process and sometimes, when there is a fork in the road, you might take the wrong path.
Some events in life are difficult to write about. We wanted everything to
be perfect, but that is not to be. In reading old letters I had written to my

parents, while in the army in Indonesia, and eventually returned to me, I realized, that from a historical prospective, they contain omissions, probably to not to upset my parents. But by omitting these events from a story, it would be impossible to get an accurate picture of life in another country. A case in point is the break up of two marriages, those of Alan and Glenn. We cannot go into many details, as we lived out of their private lives, and we can only talk about things in which we personally were involved.

Both marriages were of relative short duration. Alan and his wife bought a house and moved in. Then a baby girl was born, but before long the mother moved out with the baby and moved in with her widowed mother. Eventually the whole family went to court lending support and after a series of court appearances, this ended in divorce. It did not help that the female lawyer seemed to have a hate for men, making it impossible to get proper representation. Then another lawyer came on the scene, specializing in family law, and was able to straighten everything out. The opposition was very intimidated by the presence of all our family members. Then Alan met a dietitian of Scottish descent. Janet Macdonald became the daughter we never had. Both were to have very successful careers. Alan became a real estate appraiser and they both bought a beautiful home.

The other marriage was that of Glenn. The family was British and the father of the bride was a British Army Major, in Canada to teach at a community college. This short liaison resulted in a baby as well this time a boy, and here again, the immature mother left for her parents' house. Again, we went to court with the whole family and there we learned that the parents of the mother had already a foster parent lined up in British Columbia, willing to adopt the baby. Immediately, Lydie and I said to each other "No Way!". I stood up and declared in front of the judge, that we would adopt the baby and immediately the judge reacted with: "That's within the family, and I agree", and instantly the case was closed. The other grand parents were furious, and decided, that we were not to pick up the baby ourselves, with the result, that another social worker from Lydie's office picked up the baby and brought him to us, a bit down the road in front of a church, where we were waiting in the car to receive him.

Lydie's colleagues declared us crazy, after all, who in his or her right mind would adopt a baby, when retirement is relatively close by. "At your age? Why would anybody want a diaper baby?" But then, after a while, they said to her: "You have a spring in your step, since you adopted a child!" They knew, that when they would retire, they would have an empty house, while we would still have a young one and bringing his friends.

Now we needed a baby crib, diapers, and everything connected with this new life, but then, we had gone through this three times, and we were ready for a new challenge. I had to go to the post office to pick up a form to apply for Family Allowance. The postmaster was standing behind the counter when I came into the room. Then I dropped my request, and saw his face show that he was puzzled. "Family Allowance?", he asked. He did not say, what he was obviously thinking: "My goodness man, at your age? For eighteen years, he was our son, and we decided that the time had come for Glenn to re-adopt his son. Now it was the lawyer who was puzzled. "Re-adopt? That is never done, but it must be possible somehow". Patrick was now our grandson again. We were ready for a new challenge and we took it and in the process, we extended our own youth by eighteen years. The whole family benefited from this decision and we certainly benefited the most.

CHAPTER TWENTY-THREE

LYDIE IN COURT

Lydie entered the Provincial building in Saint John and quickly took the elevator to the third floor, where the courtrooms were located. It was not to be a trial this time, but just an examination of discovery. A couple was charged with child abuse and the prosecutor needed to find out if enough evidence was available to proceed further. Lydie worked on many abuse cases, and this one would not be any different from most of them. When she entered the courtroom, she noticed that the lawyer for the defense was already sitting at a table flanked by her clients. Lydie looked at the judge's bench, under the portrait of the Queen, the thermos can with water and at the recorder's desk. Then she heard "all rise" and the judge entered the courtroom and they could proceed.

Lydie thought back when Glenn was a one-year-old baby. Glenn had developed many bruises on his arms, legs and on his head. One arm was swollen and in the emergency department of the hospital, he was examined and the doctor suspected child abuse. After a day's tests, the doctor apologized, because he had discovered that Glenn was a hemophiliac. The judge, an older man, was very dignified in court. He called her Mrs. von Weiler, but when the audience left, he often called her in for a chat. Now it was "Lydie, could you come into my office for a minute?". He had fought with the Canadian troops in Holland and was always eager to talk about his favourite foreign country.

The judge started to speak. In the Court of Queen's bench of New Brunswick, the Minister of the Department of Health and Welfare versus John and Brenda W.. First witness to testify on behalf of the Crown is Lydie von Weiler, Social worker for the Department of Health and Welfare of Saint John. After having been duly sworn in, Lydie was exam ined by the counsel for the defense. And now lawyer Lynda H. started to ask questions about her qualifications, her experiences in the past and her education in Holland and the social work she did. She was trying to find ways to discredit her in the hope to find a reason to bolster her case. But her adversary was well prepared, was never lost for words, and was prepared for a fishing expedition, which did not get very far. Question: "In 1976 when you worked for the Alcohol Rehabilitation Centre as a coun-selor, did that position involve working inside the rehabilitation centre itself, providing counseling to the inmates, is that what you were doing? Answer: "That is right" Lydie's mind went back to that period, and she thought about the time, that she found beer bottles in the water tank of the toilet in the washroom and how ironic it was that the building in which the center was located was now a pizza restaurant with a bar.

The questions went back to the position she held now and she had to explain her duties and responsibilities. Her caseload was extensive and it involved situations, where she had to take children in protective care and a great deal of administrative work, was something she had to do, but would have rather given to the administrative staff, but it was a part of what she had to do. The court was so impressed with the quality of her reports that more often, she was asked by the judges to make reports, which did not sit well with her colleagues, who felt being passed over by the courts. Now the lawyer, realizing that she could not find anything in this social worker's background, which could be used against her in this case, she started to ask questions about the case itself. Question: "Has there been ever a time, Mrs. von Weiler, when you have felt that you not want to proceed with a protective care or you would not want to proceed on a matter when your decision has been overruled by your superiors and you've had to proceed or ultimately is your decision as an outworker re-spected by your superiors? Do you understand what I'm saying?" Answer: "Yes, I'm just trying to think. No. I can't say that ever happened; not that I can remember...to the best of my knowledge, I mean, I have about eight years in there now, you know". Question: "Okay, hard to remember every case that comes up the pipe. What generally speaking would be your routine when you investigate these cases? How do you investigate a case which involves allegations of sexual and physical abuse?" Answer: "Again, in general, because there always exceptions to the rule, but in general, we interview the child first. This is really, more or less, a rule except if you cannot do so because of certain circumstances in the home and it also depends on the age of the child. Now the lawyer was fishing again, trying desperately to catch her off guard, but it did not seem to work. Question: "If you came into information, which led you to believe that professionals and I'm talking about psychologists, physicians, may be even psychiatrists have been involved in a family-in-trouble, for a period of time, would you contact these people to find out what their involvement had been and what the problem was? Answer: Yes, but there is a difference between these professionals and neighbours. I would not contact the neighbours." Question:" Now you are brought here today to bring with you, your file and the file of the Department with respect to the Department's action against my clients?

Answer: "Yes" Lydie knew that the Defense counsel would now get into details of the case.

She would try to interrogate Lydie, as if she herself was on trial, but the next hour or so, she would be cool and collected, because she had done her homework. She would not be intimidated, nor would she be a victim of trick questions by a lawyer on a fishing expedition. She knew what to do, and, as usual, whatever the outcome, the Judge would agree whatever was recommended. It was all in a day's work

When we talk about judges, we should not forget a strange experience I had with a lawyer. When one of the most respected and senior barristers in the city, Benjamin Guss, Q.C. (Queens Counsel) and a criminal lawyer, phoned me one day, to tell me that he needed to see me, the first thought came up that I must be in some kind of trouble, although I did not have any idea what that might be. When I visited his office and sat in front of his large mahogany desk, he revealed quickly that it was he, who was in trouble. He told me that he was appointed consul for the Netherlands and he had absolutely no idea what the function entailed. Saint John did not have a consul for five years, and the Consul-General in Montreal had sent him a steamer trunk. He stared at the box and after I congratulated him on his appointment, I suggested that we open the trunk. A number of Dutch emigrants lived in the Sussex area and it was estimated that people of Dutch descent might be in the four percent range. The port was a place of call for a number of Dutch shipping lines as well as Canadian lines calling on Amsterdam and Rotterdam, indicating that the consul could provide valuable services to the Netherlands.

We opened the trunk. I did not let on, that I was equally as curious as he was. First he lifted out an old and very dusty portrait of Queen Juliana. I told him, that while a new queen was in power, he might clean it and find the portrait a place in his office until a new and more recent one arrived. The second item was an oval shield, indicating that this was now a consulate. I told him to hang it outside the building, preferable over the front door.

"Would the owner of the building object?" he wondered, "On the contrary, it would bring prestige to the building", I answered. "And then the rent will go Up" he added quickly. Obviously he was thinking that perhaps this prestigious appointment would cost him money. Next item out of the trunk was an old card file in a little box, which had cards with Dutch names and addresses of people who probably had moved away. It was obvious that this trunk had not been opened for a long time. A box of pencils, hardly used, an eraser, a moth eaten Dutch flag, a receipt book and old newspapers, magazines, letterheads of the former consul and yellow on the edges. And then he took out a seal. "Oh, I recognize that" he exclaimed, "but what is it used for, I wonder...passports perhaps? The last item he picked up fell on the floor, an old school scribbler with expense notes:

```
Five stamps @ $0.15 .... $0.75
Receipt book ................ $0.85
Telegram...................... $1.36
Envelops ...................... $1.39
```

There was also a notation not to forget to send an expense statement to External Affairs in The Hague at the end of the month. Appointing the highest paid lawyer in the city to the Office of Honorary Consul to the Netherlands was the best deal the frugal folks at External Affairs could have made.

CHAPTER TWENTY-FOUR

BRIAN

Brian seemed happy in that Cheshire home, as he had all the help he needed. In the morning, he was picked up with a wheelchair bus and went to work. Yet, he was still looking for a bit more independence, and he found one in a nearby town. In Burlington was an apartment tower, and now the owners had one floor set aside for the wheelchair bound. One apartment became an office, where attendants were being dispatched to help the residents. The apartments now had wider doors and other amenities like a telephone system whereby one only had to dial a one-digit number to ask for an attendant. 1-I want to get up, 2- I want to take a bath, 3- I want breakfast, 4- please clean up the room, etc. It was on the eleventh floor. Being alone was different, of course, but then Glenn came, moved in with him, and was offered to be an attendant and now he was paid to look after his brother. He would earn less than his brother, who worked for an investment dealer, but it was a start. They put a bed in the living room, which made the apartment look smaller, but it worked out for them. They bought a second hand wheelchair van and now Brian was even more independent. They enjoyed living in the city.

Max, the cat, was sitting on the windowsill, baking in the sun, as usual. The fresh air blew in his nose from the open window and he licked his whiskers. When he was looking down, he saw the heavy traffic passing the building. The clanging of the streetcar bells kept this tomcat awake. He had long forgotten his last home at the animal shelter, but that was long ago. Life was good. There was food in the kitchen, a choice of beds to sleep on and the windowsill in the sun. Could a cat ask for more? One morning after breakfast, Brian and Glenn left for work. The dishes were left in the sink; these could wait for their return. The cat looked at the faucet, which showed one drop of water coming every once in a while. The droplets fell on a half submersed cup up side down in the water, which sounded like tick, tick. This made him thirsty, and he tried to jump on the counter. After a few tries, he succeeded when he jumped via the furniture and landed safely. Now he had to walk on the edge near the sink, carefully, not to fall, then with his out stretched paw, he pushed the long faucet handle, and now hot water came out and, now frightened, he jumped off the counter onto the floor and took cover under the bed. When Brian and Glenn returned, an hour and a half after Max's scare, they arrived at the apartment door, where the carpet was wet. Glenn entered the apartment and then he entered a sauna. He ran to the faucet to turn it off, but bumped twice against the furniture as the fog hindered his eyesight. Ten centimeters of water had to be disposed off immediately. They called the superintendent, who came with a dry and wet vacuum and together they worked hard to clean it all up. Then Glenn went with him to the three apartments below to do the same thing. When all was done, it was quiet in the apartment once more. Max came out of his hiding place, still a bit scared; he took up his place on the windowsill.

Soon Glenn was working for the same firm, Brian was working for, and they moved up in very responsible positions. Glenn became Account receivables Manager collecting millions of dollars and Brian became Executive Assistant and office manager. Patrick telephoned Glenn every Saturday night and visited him during the summer holidays, and on a long Labour Day weekend. They used their holidays to start traveling all over North America. They saw more of this continent than we ever did. Patrick went with them and he too had incredible experiences but eventually, they longed for their family and decided to return home. The owners of the company they worked for did everything to keep them, but to no avail. They asked us to look for an apartment, and we found one that was suitable, and they returned. We were a bit worried, because unemployment was high again, and it would be hard to find work, but when we brought up the subject, the answer was clear. "We are looking for a house to buy. Then we take six months off to make it accessible and then we are not looking for a job. "Not looking for a job?" we asked. "No, we are going to start a business", "What kind of business?" we asked "Carpet cleaning" was the answer. We told them that there were many such companies in the yellow pages of the telephone book. "But they don't know how to sell themselves". They proved us wrong. Eventually they had four thousand clients and a number of other companies fell by the wayside.

After renting very expensive machines, they bought one and now the cost was going down. They hired personnel to help Glenn, but that turned out to be costly, because they were slow and lazy. They found that January and February were months, during which nobody needed their services, it seemed, and therefore they closed down the business during that period and spent these months in Florida or California and later they would visit New York, Atlantic City, Las Vegas or Washington. Each year the business grew by fifty percent, but some years, that percentage was much higher. They did some commercial jobs, but it was usual, that they had to wait 30 days for their money, that is why they decided to stick with residential jobs. Glenn has a natural ability for public relations, which was a large part of their success. One night, he phoned me. His helper had called in sick, and he needed a replacement and he asked me of I could help him for the day, which I did. Around six o'clock in the evening we went to a house and we unloaded all the pails and hoses, machine and soaps and he started doing the main floor of a house. Usually, he worked from upstairs down to downstairs, and when he reached the basement rooms, he asked me to put most of the materials back into the truck. I went out of the side door with a pail and a hose and since it was now dark, I was confused, where the truck was. Instead of turning right after leaving the building, I turned left with the result that I fell into the swimming pool. It had a floating blanket and now I was on top of that floating blanket, trying to throw the hose and the pail on the side, while I was slowly sinking. Then when I crawled out, I was dripping all over. I went back, passing the side door and opened it and called for Glenn. He came out and laughed so hard, that I had to tell him to be quiet, because I did not want the owner to see what I had done. I also was concerned of making the truck seat all wet, but he said that he didn't mind. When we were back home I told Lydie of my misfortune, and she laughed, because the client was a colleague of hers.

In November 1997, all our lives were shattered, when Brian died. I wrote a long letter to the family in Holland. It was a moment that we missed them most. It was now, that we needed support the most, but we had to find the strength within ourselves. "Although the postal employees are on strike here, we want to take this opportunity to write a letter to be mailed when the service starts again. On Sunday, November 9th our children and grandchildren were invited for dinner on the occasion of Brian's 41st birthday, but on Saturday, Glenn phoned us to tell that Brian had a rash on his behind, from sitting down too much and in addition, he did not feel well. So the dinner was postponed for a while. On Sunday we went to Brian and Glenn to bring a birthday present. Glenn told us that the next morning, he would phone the family doctor and when he did, he talked to his secretary she told him that the doctor would never make house calls and that he better bring him in. He did and the doctor said that he did not want to play nurse and that he better go to the out patient department of the hospital where they would fix him up. He did that and there a doctor on call looked Brian over and did some tests and said that he had a lot of liquid in his stomach. They decided that, in order to do more tests, he would be better off to be admitted. Tuesday morning, we went to the hospital and he was in a good mood. His mouth had too much liquid, which was a bother and swallowing became a bit hard. Glenn was present and after we visited him for quite some time, we met the attending physician who told us, that what he needed was extra oxygen, to help him breathe. He also told us that might be permanent. He asked us if he could be honest with Brian and we said, that he would want that very much. We went home, while Glenn stayed at the hospital. Before dinner, Glenn called us to tell us that Brian was going to intensive care. He decided not to go home, but stay with Brian as long as needed. After supper, we were on the telephone, when the doorbell rang. There was a policeman and also David Leadley, a colleague of Lydie and a friend of us. Alan apparently had called the police and Janet had called David, whose wife was a colleague of hers at the hospital.

We went immediately to the hospital and when we arrived at the intensive care department, we first met Glenn and then Alan and Janet, who came immediately towards us. They told us that Brian had died. Lisa and

Patrick were there as well and it was a very emotionally scene in the waiting room next door. Because Janet was an Anglican, she had asked Father Allen to come over, just for support. He was a very kind and compassionate person. It was hard on the children, especially Lisa, Alan's daughter and Patrick, Glenn's son. Then, one after the other, we went next door to say good-bye to Brian. For Patrick this was very difficult. Then Lydie and I drove home. Lydie, who was driving, then stopped on the side of the road, which was surrounded by woods. It was too much for her. After a while we continued our trip home.

On Wednesday, we went to the funeral home. The director was an old friend and also a Kiwanian. Alan, Janet, Glenn, Lydie and I were all present. We had arranged that a grief counselor and a friend as well, would take Patrick out for a while on the same day. She was specialized in grief management for kids. This was exactly what was needed and it helped Patrick a great deal. He was to be cremated and his ashes spread on our little lake near our house, the one Brian loved so much and could sit for hours in his wheelchair looking out at the birds in and near the water. Patrick did not go to school the rest of the week. On Friday we had an open house at Alan and Janet's home. We had made a collage of Brian's photo's on the mantel piece and many visitors, when they looked at the pictures, noted that on each picture he was smiling, a fact we had noticed that before ourselves. Many of the visitors brought cakes and snacks, something we did not expected, it seemed a tradition here. The reception was to be from 6pm-9pm but around seven, it started to snow and the roads became very treacherous. A number of guests did not make it, they could not go up the slippery hill near Alan and Janet's home. There were notices in the paper and many cards arrived after the mail strike was over. After a while, Glenn went working again, but for the first week, he did not want to enter Brian's room.

Then, on a Saturday, he had supper in the city with Alan and the two were together for hours. They decided to do this more often. Later he had supper with us. He told us that he now sleeps the whole night through, something he could not do for the last eight years. Brian called him often in the middle of the night to be turned around or to go to the bathroom. Now he has work for two. His two employees were a great help, but still a lot came upon his shoulder, because Brian was very knowledgeable administrator and knew about the law and the taxes. We received many cards and telephone calls and even e-mail messages from former students at the university Brian went to. When Brian and Glenn went on their holiday trips to sunny places, he now knows, that if he wanted to do that, he had to go alone. "Brian was not only my brother, but my best friend", he told us.

We are always concerned for Glenn, because for the last many years, he had hardly a social life. For eight years, life was his care for Brian, and all that lifting caused more bleeding in his knees, with the result, that he needed artificial knees and now they look at his ankles. It is a fact that the care for Brian all those years is affecting his health for years to come. On the one hand, we are grateful, but our concern will never go away. Patrick suggested that we plant a Hawthorne tree next to the lake in Brian's memory. We asked permission from the town, because it owned the park and it was granted. The whole family was present when we planted the tree. Now each spring it is full of white blossoms.

CHAPTER TWENTY-FIVE

ALAN

Our concern for our oldest son was of a different nature. Our attention had to be focused on the other two, because they had physical problems, we tried to solve in some fashion. We were constantly very well aware, that due to the circumstances, attention to Alan might well have been somewhat lacking. This was probably one reason why we decided to give Alan a ticket to Holland for his 16th birthday. We felt that he deserved something special. He flew to Holland and stayed with his grandfather, who gave him a pass on the train. And he visited Jaap, Flory and Rudolf and their families and he even visited the silver factory. He had his day in the sun and the family members took him in as their own son. Alan loved to travel and a year later, he joined the navy cadets and took a navy vessel up the coast of Newfoundland and Labrador for seven weeks. In the fall he started university, followed by Brian, a year later. Brian had a problem there, because the buildings were hardly accessible to wheelchairs. The campus was laid out as a series of two story blocks, connected with corridors. Each block had another level and could be accessed by climbing three steps. Students took turns to move him. He also studied a great deal in the library.

Alan ran for a seat on the school board and went through the political process with canvassing, pamphlets, ballots and signs. He lost the race, but he gained valuable experience. That summer Flory visited us enroute to our family members in Detroit, where she had been invited to visit by my father's younger brother Willem. The same year, Alan was accepted into the International exchange program Canada World Youth.

After a month's training in Moncton, he left for Quebec, where he was to meet Mexican and other students taking part at Camp Edvi. He learned Spanish and how to get along with others. After a while, they were put into a farmhouse for more training. After a few weeks, he hitchhiked home for a few days and then returned to Quebec, where they all went by plane to Burnaby, British Columbia. Alan worked in a day care centre there, was given all the required needles to go to Mexico and left for the last part of his adventure. Just before Christmas he flew home and with him was a Mexican student. Maria Theresa Gonzalez Lorero, stayed with us during Christmas and the New Years Eve. On New Year's Day it had snowed and the next Saturday they would leave for Mexico. It was impossible to bring them to the highway, because now the road was covered with six feet of snow. Maria, who had never seen snow, indicated that she was not to go through that experience.

But Alan put snowshoes on and showed her how to walk on top of the snow. They walked to the highway, which was plowed. They hitch hiked into town, where Alan left his two pairs of snowshoes after they took a bus to the airport for the voyage to Mexico. On their arrival in Mexico City, they were driven to a Boy Scouts camp, where they stayed for a few days to get used to the climate. It had snowed there as well. With an old dilapidated bus, they left for a small village, where they lived among very poor people in huts. After four months, Alan returned with the other students and arriving at the airport, they learned that the airport tax had not been paid. They walked up and down the airport terminal until they found a friendly Texan who paid the tax for them.

When Alan returned from Mexico, he had another girl with him, Andrea. Her parents had a farm in Ontario and she studied French. The two decided to take their backpacks and hike through Europe for a few weeks, which was the in-thing at the time. They had passes on the train and went to Holland to visit our family and then to Switzerland, Italy, Greece and France before returning to Holland. Family members loved the two and Grandfather Arnold hoped secretly, that she would become a member of the family, but it was not meant to be. While Alan was in Holland, we decided to sell the house. It had become difficult to navigate Brian in and out of the house and we thought, that a bungalow style house would be much better. We had lived in that house for eight years. The children grew up there and they had all the pets they ever wanted, but they were older now and times had changed.

A month after Alan and Andrea returned, Lydie and I left for a holiday in Holland as well and we were there for three weeks. We had just left a trying time behind us. Glenn had pain in his groin one day and we took him to Dr. Robb. He put his finger on the painful spot and let go. Glenn screamed and Doug said: "Clearly appendicitis". Glenn left for the hospital, was given massive doses of Factor 8 and was operated on. After the operation, the hematologist said: "I never ever saw such a thing; I never saw a drop of blood". Alan had a job at a bank and while Lydie and I were in Holland, he took the car to do a field-call. Glenn was driving and they just had their seatbelts on. When they backed up on a driveway, they hit a hole in the road and the car flipped upside down into a ditch. The luggage rack on the roof acted as some kind of sleigh. Most of the windows were broken and the car on the outside heavily damaged. When they smelled gas, they quickly scrambled out of the windows to a safe place. Alan phoned the police and they took the boys home. Alan went to the insurance company to settle the claim and the car was written off. Since the insurance company was now the owner of the car, Alan asked the insurance adjuster: "How much to you want for the car?" "Two or three hundred dollars", was the answer. Alan decided to buy the car back. He drove it to a gas station to check the fluids and then he drove it home. "Where is the car?" I asked, when we arrived back from our trip. "It is a bit damaged", he replied, "But here is a cheque for you". We drove the car for another six months.

With the help of a university professor, Alan started a company, incorporated and started a pizza store with Brian and Glenn. The idea was to get business experience, since they took a business administration course, and to earn money for university. They were very successful, but in the fall when university started up again, they found it very hard to run a business and study at the same time. They also experienced that, in their absence, the quality of the pizza's made by employees went down and the business started to fall off. Glenn did the deliveries and Brian looked after the financial part. It was a real partnership. The store was called

Mr. Pizza. Meanwhile, we sold the house in Hammond River and bought a house in the Stoneycroft subdivision in Quispamsis. Before we bought the house, we rented a basement apartment nearby, while looking for a suitable home. It was there that Glenn fell out of a tree. We had planned to go out for dinner in a restaurant in town and Glenn had made reservations. Just before we left, he came into the house in a daze. We asked him, if he had ordered a table and he asked "What table?". We realized that something was wrong and immediately we left for the hospital. He had another bleeding in his head. The dinner was off, but Glenn was fine after a few days.

"How can I get experience, if, in the whole province nobody will hire me without it?", Janet asked a prospective employer. Janet Macdonald was surprised, that after getting a degree, and now a full-fledged dietitian, and after serving an internship, it was impossible to get work. She applied to other provinces and then was offered a job in Saint John, New Brunswick. She joined the Regional hospital staff. Now she could get the experience and after a while, she would return, perhaps to her home town London, Ontario., where her parents lived. Her sister Penny, who had a degree in entomology, would never have that problem, she thought. Alan found it hard to meet people during the years following his divorce. His life was taken up with work, this time at a furniture store and his daughter Lisa every other weekend and a little time for social activities.

But then his luck changed when he met Janet. They met in a wine bar and ten months later Alan bought an engagement ring, just before Valentine's Day. He borrowed Glenn's car and tied the ring onto a string of a balloon and on Valentine's Day he planned to pop the question. At the last minute he changed his mind about the balloon and bought a box of chocolates. He wrapped the ring in gold foil and placed it between the chocolates in the centre of the box. While driving to Janet's apartment with a bottle of wine and the box of chocolates, and the balloon, he had a flat tire. He went to a gas station to pump up the tire, when all of a sudden, he saw the balloon in the air. What luck, the ring was not going into the air with it! That summer they went to Holland to meet the family, and, not surprisingly, Janet felt immediately at home. She did not get used to the interviews by Grandfather Arnold and Rudolf, but the family took her in immediately. After a visit to Paris, they returned to Saint John to make plans for their wedding. In the history of Scotland, the Clan Donald was the most powerful of all highland clans. While Janet was born in Canada, her Scottish heritage is ever present. The Scots have one thing in common with the Dutch; they are all fiercely independent. Alan and Janet think strongly about their roots.

While Janet visited Scotland with her mother, she met her distant cousins. After being there for a while, she did not realize that she was beginning to sound like these relatives as well, then, someone said to her: "You almost lost your Canadian accent". Alan had a Dutch passport for a while until he lost his dual citizenship, due to age limitations. He was still to own a bit of Holland, as he owned a share in the family farm Polder Jannezand. In many ways Alan and Janet complement each other.

CHAPTER TWENTY-SIX

TRYING TO CHANGE

With one member of the family in need of using a wheel chair, it became evident how little New Brunswick was prepared for the disabled. We expected quite a number of families having the same problems as we did. Teenagers becoming adults, and nobody around to do the physical help they needed. We certainly were not able to lift him anymore. A friend of mine and I started an organization to try to change things for the better. We had a first meeting in a church basement and we were surprised how many wheelchair bound people came to that meeting, just after one ad in the paper. Before they could be admitted to the meeting, we had to make that church accessible in the first place, which showed that we had an additional problem. We incorporated and were able to get some grants, we hired an architect, and we built a group home, and a year later we built a second one. We operated these homes with success and we never had any vacancies. The idea to sign for mortgages was at first somewhat daunting, but we were incorporated; they would never go after individuals. After the operation closed due to changes in policy by the government, we learned that they could have gone after individuals after all. We had a lot of help, from other organizations and were able to furnish these facilities adequately.

Over time, the need arose for transportation, not only for the residences, operated under the name C.O.I.L Inc. "Centres Offering Independent Lifestyles", but other citizens were also in need of wheelchair buses, and we bought a few and started an operation from one of the group homes. That was successful too, but we started to realize that that operation was getting expensive, and the maintenance cost and fuel was giving us a headache. I went to the manager of City Transit. I mentioned that the subsidies he received from various governments were for service of all the citizens, but that 4% of them cannot use city buses to travel with, due to mobility problems. "So you want 4% of all the subsidies we get", he replied. And I answered: "Of course not", and now he was all ears, and wondered, what was coming down the pipe. "You have employees, who are mechanics in your garage. I venture to say, that there will be times that they have little to do. Could they use that time to have a look at our wheelchair vans? Now, that sounded reasonable; it also would bypass the budget sheet. "And while we're at it, could we tank at your pump? "

We were trying to solve two other problems. One was accessibility and the other was handicap parking. There was a church in town that had a very wide granite stairway up to the front doors and a neon sign indicating that everyone is welcome. I went to the pastor and commented on that sign. "Too bad it is not accurate", I said, four percent of the citizens are not welcome, because they cannot get up the stairs with their wheel chairs. In a week he phoned me to tell me that the church now had a ramp to the side door and I congratulated him. It seemed I was getting notorious, because I received a telephone call from an architect, designing the new General Hospital. He wanted me to look at the plans and after one look I had a question: "What is that?" "Is that a coffee shop hanging on the ceiling?" He told me that he always wanted to do something like that". I told him that even pregnant mothers are pushed sitting in wheelchairs, partly for insurance purposes. Wheelchairs were not welcome in the cafeteria, it seemed, but he did not change his plans, except for some slight alterations. Thus, the cafeteria was built. I also told him that before the opening, he should sit in a wheelchair and be pushed by an orderly. He should have his secretary follow him to make notes and he was to check every room, all the light switches and the height of counters in the washrooms. He did that and afterward, he phoned me, telling me that he found $12,000 dollar's worth of changes that had to be made.

We collected by-law statutes from several cities in the country, which had instituted handicap parking. We made a presentation to city council, but they only had one objection. Commercial plazas and shopping centres are privately owned and the city cannot force them to make handicap parking spots available. I showed them that many cities found ways to bypass that problem. The city bought handicap signs and set a fines program, and we were in business. In the process the citizens became very much aware of the plight of the mobility impaired and now, building codes have been altered to include measures to make public buildings accessible and now people are not parking on handicap parking spaces anymore, perhaps partly due to the $80 fines.

CHAPTER TWENTY-SEVEN

BI-CENTENNIAL

One day, in 1984, I was walking outside on my lunch break, and passed the Tourist office, when I saw a sign indication that it now had an office of the upcoming Bi-Centennial committee working on next years' festivities. Wondering, what they were up to, I dropped in to have a look. There I talked to the newly appointed executive Director, Peter Garner, who was interested in talking to me. He asked me what I was doing, because, coming from Ontario, he did not yet meet too many people here. Before I knew it, I became a member of the committee. Now I was wondering how much work that would entail, and if I had time to do what was asked of me. I still was busy producing the employees magazine for the telephone company, wrote press releases and did other public relations work, but this could run into my time. Now I attended every Wednesday a meeting at his office at lunchtime, and the City brought in coffee and sandwiches.

After my fourth meeting, Peter Garner said: "We met four times now and they were absolutely non productive and we still don't have any plans. If you cannot come up with any, you can go home and I will appoint another committee who can. Then I dropped the bomb that exploded all around me. "Since it will be 1985, it coincides with the 40th anniversary of the liberation of the Netherlands after the Second World War, perhaps we can bring in a choir from Holland". "Everybody think this is good idea?", Peter asked and all committee members nodded their heads "Everybody agrees that Joost will organize this?" and again everybody nodded. Now I was trapped and I did not have the foggiest notion how to proceed, and then I left for the office with a big problem on my hands.

Fortunately, the telephone company was anxious for me to do this, as it showed that the company had a great interest in the City, in other words, it would be good public relations. I wrote to an association of choirs in Holland and they contacted the most suitable choir organization and it was not long, before I received a letter from its secretary of the choir that they were interested. In addition they found a sponsor. They were from Aalsmeer, a town close to Amsterdam, which was famous for its gigantic flower auction co-op. They decided to send an advance party to Saint John to look us over. They came one day, laden with flowers for the mayor and for me and when they arrived I escorted them to a motel, which I had arranged for them to use. Their initial impression was one of disbelief, that I could pull this off as the choir would sent 108 people, all of which had to be billeted. They asked me hundreds of questions, and after I helped the men with their suitcases into the rooms, one person put the television on, and was very surprised, to see me on TV talking about the choir with a minister who was interested in choirs. I was explaining to him what the plans were going to be and now it seemed that all doubts faded away. But even I did not know what problems I had to solve, nor what I was getting into. The Mayor received the guests and before they left again, they had one bouquet left over, which they gave to the chambermaid of the motel, who started to cry, because nobody ever had given her flowers before.

The choir was to fly to Halifax and with buses they would drive to Saint John. Many members would bring their wives and I needed 108 beds for a week. When I talked to a concert organizer, he gave me his opinions. "This is crazy", he said, "It can't be done. In the first place, you never find people opening their houses for 108 foreigners and then for a full week. When are they giving their concert?" he wanted to know. "They are giving two large concerts, one in a church and the other in a theatre, then they are giving mini concerts in a Veteran's hospital and in a senior's complex, then they sing at two malls..."Wait a minute", he interrupted "Two paid concerts and a number of free ones? You have no idea what you are doing. In the first place you cannot fill two halls by the same group in one week and then all these free concerts, it is going to be a colossal disaster". Now I was getting worried and I decided not to tell him, that it was now four days before they would arrive and I had already four families with beds. I went to the newspaper to drop off a strong worded letter to the editor and back in the car, I thought "should I take it back, it was too strong, but I decided against it. After the paper came out, the telephone in our house started ringing off the hook and at midnight I received a call from an irate woman who had tried all night, but our phone was always busy. Within a day, I had my quota and I had the foresight to take more calls, in case some would fall off, which actually happened.

The manager of a car rental agency I was acquainted with was standing in the door opening, taking in the warmth of a spring morning. I was passing by in a hurry and waved at him and he called me back. "I hear you are bringing in a choir from Holland for the Bi-Centennial celebrations, how many people are coming?" he asked, "108", I replied. "That means they are bringing in 108 suitcases and sixty zipper-bags with suits and sixty bouquet of flowers for their billeting hosts", I added and I did not have any clue what he was talking about. "Do you still drive that little two door Toyota hatchback car?" "of course", I answered. "What you need is a Magic Wagon", and I said "What I need is more money, which I don't have in my budget" Then he offered me a van for a week and the only stipulation was that I would fill up the gas tank, before I would return the vehicle. Later in the day I visited an elderly couple, who asked me to inspect what they had to offer. It turned out that they gave the guests their own bedroom.

Then I received a call from Chicago from a woman, who was apparently working for the big Flower Auction Co-op in Aalsmeer. She told me that she was a flower arranger and every year she worked on the Rose Bowl Parade in Pasadena, California with floats as large as two school buses but now she was working on a convention. "I am coming over for half a week and in a few days, you have to pick up from the airport in Saint John a planeload of cut flowers and this is what I want you to do. In the first place, I need a room in a central hotel. You look after that. Then I want you to find a cold storage building and ask the manager for a cool space where I can work, a table, and a faucet, which I can use to get water. Do you have that so far?" "Yes Ma'am", I said, "Next you borrow 100 pails and when you have the pails, you take the flowers, cut two centimeters off the bottom of the stems put these in the pails and bring them to the cool storage place. I want you to pick me up from the airport, and bring me to my hotel and then I do not want you to contact me for a couple of days and then I will call you" "You have all that?" "Yes Ma'am", I answered. What have I done, I thought, now I'm in a real fix! Where do I get all those pails? When do I have time for all this? At work, at my department of the Telephone Company, I was telling my story. Then, out of the blue, I was told to take all the time off I needed. They regarded this as part of my public relations work. I was stunned, but happy. After two days, the woman called me again, now from Saint John. "What transportation do you have?" "I have a Magic Wagon?" I answered. "You don't have any idea what I have been doing here, do you. Some of the pieces I have made will have to be carried by three strong men. And you need and open three ton truck, because they are over a meter high." Then before she was leaving again, she called me and I dreaded hearing from her by now.

"When you have that big concert on Friday, you will have to supervise how I wanted the stage to be decorated with the flower arrangements. I made a sketch, precisely how I want to have that done. I also made a couple of corsages for the members of the choir. I want you to get volunteers to make the other fifty-eight, exactly like the samples. Then two hours before the concert I want you to get ten Boy Scouts to check all the individual flowers on stage. Even if one is wilted, I want to have it replaced by a fresh one. I want everything to be perfect and count on you to supervise all this. Now I also want you to make a list of hospitals and nursing homes and have volunteers and drivers and trucks handy after the concert to deliver all the flower arrangements to these places. Thanks for your cooperation. Now would you please pick me up at the hotel and bring me to the airport." I created a monster, which was growing day by day. This whole thing is turning into a nightmare, I thought.

The arrival and exchange of guests with the hosts at the plaza went smoothly. I did get a couple of phone calls next morning, one from a woman who asked: "You know that couple we picked up last night? They are not married" "You know madam, that can happen in the 1980's", I replied, "You don't understand", the woman continued, "We borrowed a double bed from the neighbours and now we learned that they are mother and son and they had to sleep in that double bed" "I'm sorry", I replied,

I'll be over, I have another address for the son" I answered, and then she said: " Oh, don't do that, they like it here, we borrowed another bed from the other neighbour". I was getting calls from Ontario and Quebec as well from all Atlantic Provinces from people, who wanted to fly over and wanted me to reserve tickets for them and in the end, we sold more than a thousand tickets for these concerts and the places were packed and beautifully decorated with fresh flowers.

The Dutch consul flew over from Montreal and at the last concert I was reading to the audience a telegram I received from H.M. Queen Beatrix. When they went home again, I was at the same mall where they arrived and the hosts said good byes to their guests. Then, when they had left, the mall doors were locked behind me, I went to my car and sat there for fifteen minutes, glad it was all over, in fact the only thought that came to me was "it was quite a venture and it turned out well, but I will never do it again." But that was wishful thinking, because, as they say: Never say Never! In fact, five years later, in 1990, I was busy repeating the same event, but now we would fly to Holland and this one was different.

In the many years following the Bi-Centennial, something happened, that was unexpected. Canadians, who had billeted people from the choir, exchanged birthday, anniversary and condolences cards, and took holidays to Holland and stayed with their billeting guests. Dutch choir members took their families to Saint John and visited the choir billeting hosts, and this yearly exchange was to go on for over twenty years. It was in Spring 1990 that I was at it again.

When I arrived at the church, I heard singing. The Men of Fundy were probably rehearsing for another concert. This was the choir, who five years earlier billeted members of the Dutch "Con Amore" choir, who sang a welcome song at their arrival; and helped out and even did some singing at a number of occasions. Then I received a letter from Aalsmeer. "We are organizing the 45th anniversary of the liberation of Holland and we would like the Men of Fundy to take part. We look after their billeting and organize everything if you can find ways to get them here". When I entered the church hall the conductor was just suggesting they would take a coffee break. "Do you remember the Bi-Centennial five years ago?" I asked. That was a dumb question; it was something they would never forget. The past five years they kept in touch with their newly found Dutch friends and some went to Aalsmeer already for a visit. "Would you be interested in going to Holland and stay with your Dutch friends of the Con Amore choir? I asked and I knew the answer. Then I remembered what I thought, when I saw the buses leave the mall for Halifax and the trip home, five years ago. "It was difficult, but a great success, but I don't ever do that again". But this one was to be different, as others did most of the work. In the end Lydie and I together with the men of Fundy left in late April 1990 for Holland and Aalsmeer.

They had a full program with dinners and entertainment, some small concerts, visits to the flower auction and a boat trip. In the front of the wall of the town hall of Aalsmeer was a bronze plaque commemorating the end of the Second World War and listing citizens, who had lost their lives. After a reception, where the Mayor welcomed us we were going outside for a ceremony. Children and representatives of the two choirs were there to lay wreaths and flowers and there was to be five minutes of silence and a trumpeter to play the last post. We were all standing there, the Mayor, the City council members and members of the Legion, and exactly at noon, all traffic stopped in the whole city; buses, streetcars, and people walking around; total silence. Above us, on the roof of the building, a couple of doves were scratching, and we heard rookoo, rookoo. The symbolic significance was not lost. Five minutes silence is a long time and then, all of a sudden, all church bells in the city started to ring, the traffic started up again, the trumpeter started his horn again and a small orchestra played the first verses of the national anthems of Canada and Holland and the crowd disbursed.

On Liberation day, May 5th, six buses traveled to Arnhem. It was a very hot day and on arrival, many travelers took their shoes and socks off and waded in the pool in front of city hall. Then everyone was summoned to go inside and sit on the very large steps of a stairway inside the hall where the Mayor welcomed us. He pointed at the bridge seen through the big two story tall windows, known from the film "A Bridge Too Far". Then he pointed to the Eusebius church next door, which was destroyed during the war, but was now restored to its former glory at a cost of $14 million, and then we went upstairs to a dinner sponsored by the city.

During the night, big trucks had pulled up to the church door in great secrecy. They brought thousands of yellow roses and many volunteers started to decorate the church throughout the night. These roses were especially grown for the occasion and were going to be named after the famous British songstress during the war, Vera Lynn. After our meal we walked over to the church. Lydie and I planned to sit in the middle of the church, but, when entering, we were approached by a young man, who told us told us that we had reserved seats up front. Surprised, we followed him and we were given seats in the middle of the second row. The two choirs, the Con Amoire from Aalmeer and the Men of Fundy from Saint John had already taken their seats. Now I was looking at those two choirs and all of a sudden, I realized that it all began five years earlier and that in many ways, I was responsible, which gave me a strange feeling. The rows filled up in front of us. Dame Vera Lynn came in with her husband both heavily decorated with medals and ribbons. The other dignitaries filled the row and now our row started to fill and the Mayor and his wife were sitting next to us.

Then the pipers and drums came into the church with up front a soldier holding a silver platter with one yellow "Vera Lynn" Rose, which he presented to her. Then the flags were raised and the Dutch and Canadian anthems were sung. Then the Mayor welcomed us and the concert began. Vera Lynn was not planning to sing, we learned earlier, as she had retired. At the end the Mayor spoke to thank everyone attending, which include generals, ministers, and representatives of the crown, then the Mayor ended with a line of Vera Lynn's most famous song: "Till we meet again". Then the music started to play and Vera Lynn rose out of her seat. She handed her husband her rose. All through the concert she sat like a queen, regally, with the rose on her lap, but now she walked over to the microphone, took it and then she began to sing. Now she had changed completely. Now she was the girl, singing in front of the troops, Vera Lynn, the entertainer, singing her most famous song. A tremendous emotion swept through the whole church and not a dry eye was to be seen. Now the concert had ended, but many were reluctant to leave. Many lingered to take in the beautiful roses everywhere, then, slowly they left the church.

The next day the Canadians left for the airport again and on the way it started to rain for the first time since our arrival. "See, Holland is crying, because we're leaving," these Canadians were saying. For them it was an event of a lifetime.

CHAPTER TWENTY-EIGHT

CENTENARIAN

When my father had a stroke in 1980, I left for Holland immediately, and met the family physician at the hospital, who told me, that he always said to him, if that ever happened, he did not want any part of hoses or wheelchairs, but when it did happen, his body was fighting to stay alive, and the result was that he lived another thirteen years until his death at 101. In 1992 he celebrated his 100th birthday and what a day that was. He was the centre of attention and I was reminiscing with him about my earliest experiences. One was about Sinterklaas at my elementary school.

In Holland Santa Claus is depicted as a bishop arriving with his white horse from Spain, assisted by his helper Black Peter, in Moorish costume. He has his staff with the curl on the top and Black Peter carries a burlap bag with toys, when Santa rides the rooftops sending the presents down the chimney. It is celebrated on the fifth of December. I was telling my father that I remember singing with my class outside the door of the school, in two rows, and Sinterklaas arrived by horse. My father said that he too remembered that event and after he explained to me why he remembered that day, I now could write the story, just as it happened.

"Would you mind playing Sinterklaas this year the principal of the elementary school asked my father" "We have a costume, just your size", he added. "What do you have in mind?" my father asked. "The usual thing" the principal said. "You get into your costume and we place a throne in the gym upstairs and you receive the children one by one". The prospective Sinterklaas was suspicious and sensed that the principal was leaving out a few important details. "Oh, yes, of course we'll have a white horse, that's the custom", he said casually. "A horse?", he asked, I have never been on a horse before, let alone in a get-up like this". "Don't worry so much! This horse is very tame. He is that white one belonging to the greengrocer and he has pulled the big wagon with the car wheels all his life".

My father relented and on Friday December 5th, the Feast of St. Nicholas, he reported at another parent's home just around the corner of the school. We'll help you into this costume and I think we will start with the big bishop's robe", the woman said, "My, it fits perfectly. You are going to be the best bishop ever. My father was getting a bit edgy by now. "Let's try on your miter." the woman said. "Nice colour red, don't you think? I like these red and gold bands on either side, and the gold cross in front really looks impressive."

"I am going to lose this hat for sure", Sinterklaas mumbled. The woman heard his remark and answered confidentially: "We just pin these bands with safety pins on both your shoulders and nothing serious will happen. Now, when my father cocked his head to the right, somehow, his miter moved slanted to the left. And when he moved his head to the left.... You get the idea. Here's your staff with the curl on top" she said handing him his token of dignity. "How do you expect me to steer the horse with one hand and hold the staff with the other?" He was wondering, when they stepped outside. A large white horse was tethered to the fence when Sinterklaas saw his fate, he said: "Scruffy looking, isn't he?" and then the horse and his future rider met for the first time.

The horse had one look at the person in his red bishop's robe and then he pulled his lips baring all his teeth. "See he hates me already", my father said. "Wait, where's the saddle?", he cried out. We don't have one, because the owner never had one either. He never had a rider in his life". The woman realized now that this information had been kept from Sinterklaas. "Is there anything else you didn't tell me? my father asked, but she did not answer. "How do I get on this thing", he asked, but the woman was prepared and hauled from behind the fence an old kitchen chair. "Step on this" she commanded and after a couple of tries, he was sitting on the horse, separated from him only by a grey blanket.

According to custom, he was led by Black Peter, a neighbour dressed in his Moorish costume, his face blackened. He appeared from no-where and took the reins of the horse as he walked towards the school. Sinterklaas held on to his staff, which every so often hit the side of the horse. Although he had never experienced a rider on his back, the horse instinctively knew what it meant: Go faster! He obeyed the supposed command and started to gallop. Black Peter had trouble keeping up with the horse and then Sinterklaas went around the corner toward the school.

In the meantime, all the children had lined up three rows thick on either side of the front door. The principal was standing there in front the curb, waiting to give the sign to start singing the welcome song. Then all of a sudden, Sinterklaas came racing around the corner, his staff in the air, followed by his helper, running after the horse, who decided to come to a sudden stop in front of the school. The singing just startled the horse. My father kept going forward and fell off the horse into the arms of the fright-ened principal. His staff had fallen on the sidewalk and now Sinterklaas was on his knees, feeling around for his staff, suddenly blind as a bat. His miter had moved forward and was now covering his eyes. When he felt his staff, he picked it up and stood up while he dusted off his robe. He adjusted his miter again, and all of a sudden, a hundred singing children confronted him. The children were so excited about Sinterklaas that they did not realize the disaster that had just happened. He walked between the rows of children, waving his white-gloved left hand and then made his way, following the principal into the school and to the gym upstairs. When he was seated on his throne, the children filed in one by one to visit the white-bearded visitor. When it was my turn, Sinterklaas undoubtedly asked me questions, but I did not hear what he said. I was instead looking with fascination at his shoes. "Amazing, I thought, Sinterklaas has the same shoes as my father!

I remember going to Luxembourg with my parents. I was resting under the rear window of our car driving in circles up a mountain; I saw the moon, one time left, then on the right. At the hotel kids were given pink rubber shoes to walk in the river, which had a lot of stones in it. At the river my father showed us how to skip flat stones over the water. He was really good at it.

Our biggest treat was going to the beach in Wassenaar. Mother had made bright coloured canvas shelters against the wind with bamboo poles sewn in. While we were busy making forts in the sand, we watched the shell fishermen, collecting shells using horse drawn wagons. They were dressed in red pants and blue and white striped shirts and raked the shells and scooped them into the cart, to be used to make lime. It is unthinkable to talk about my father, without including my mother, because she was not only part of a team, but also a part of him. "We can do anything we set out to do, provided we do it together" was their motto and it was proven many times to be true.

My mother could do anything that came along. Her smallish size could fool you, because, in fact, she was a tower of strength in adverse situations. One day, during the war, I came into the room and found the brown paper and fabric curtains were on fire. A corner had touched a little hotplate. The curtains were used to prevent any light from going outside, ordered by the Germans. I ran to the kitchen to get a pail of water while yelling FIRE!. Then when my mother entered the room very calmly, walking over to the chesterfield, where she grabbed a small pillow. Now she stroked the curtains in a vertical motion from top to bottom, moving to the right a pillow width every so often and the fire was out. She was the practical one, while my father was the artistic one. He made embroidery designs on paper, which my mother duplicated on tablecloths, which she embroidered. When I was in Indonesia, it was very hard on them.

During the war, they helped out a large and poor family, where the mother was bedridden. They never talked about that, but a classmate told me that my parents helped his parents out. Before my mother died, she made him promise to look after himself well. He was uncomplicated but a very compassionate man. After his stroke he lived in the home for the aged until his death. There he had all the facilities he needed and still get a quality of life he was accustomed to. He was loved by the personnel, who were always in awe at the great number of visitors he was getting every week. One older teenager visiting him asked if she could ask for advice. "Opa", you know by boyfriend, who is now at university and has one more year to go. He proposed that I would move in with him at his apartment, what do you suggest I do?" "I can give you advice, but why don't you ask your parents first? "My parents? My parents? They are so ultra conservative!" She knew that his advice was more to her liking. His thinking was years ahead of his time; always looking forward; that is why he never looked or acted his age. When he died on October 22, 1993, even in death, he did not want anybody to make a "fuss". But everybody who had crossed his path thought otherwise; and their numbers were large indeed. We all miss him.

CHAPTER TWENTY-NINE

RUDOLF, JAAP AND FLORY

On his 100th birthday, my father lamented that of his own generation nobody was alive anymore, yet he marveled at what he experienced in his life from the time of horse and buggy, to putting a man on the moon. Now, his own daughter is following in his footsteps, it seems. While she still had an active life, he was now in a wheel chair but still mentally very active. She also displayed her broad interest and love for her offspring and, now, in her early nineties, she is beginning to find herself in the same position, and more than ever, she has to attend the funerals of her friends and relatives. Like her father, always creative, producing beautiful things with her hands and her electric sewing machine, looking at art exhibitions or listening to lectures by art historians or just visiting friends, always displaying her broad interest.

The passing of two of her brothers was hitting her hard and she is hanging onto the only one she has left and when she fell and hurt her leg, she told the nurse what to do and when she disagreed about what bandages to use, she told her loudly, that a bandage should not stick to the wound, because, when you take it off, you would tear open the wound again. She loves to go to concerts with her children who show their love for her repeatedly. She studied the history of nursing in the world, and when I sent her stories of nursing in the history of Canada, she eagerly put in her collection what I sent her. It is evident, that she had the artistic talents of her father, and the ability to produce with her hands from her mother. It seems that all these talents found their way into the lives of the other siblings as well.

Rudolf was an accomplished painter, water colorist and could draw well. Although he never saw himself as a true artist, he actually was one. Jaap's talent was a bit different. When a friend brought him a box with a broken tea service, he glued everything together again, not to use, of course, but to display. He also, with a little saw, made puzzles from thin plywood and made the pieces in all kinds of form. He also was able to complete commercial puzzles, but with the picture side up side down. When his daughter became an accomplished musician playing the violin in an orchestra, he played the piano and made beautiful music with her. One of his daughters mentioned, that she often started singing with her sisters at the dinner table, what was frowned upon, but then they noticed that he was ticking with his fork against his plate in the same rhythm and when he complained, they let him know loudly.

He had quite a career during the cold war, when he was working representing a pharmaceutical company behind the Iron curtain. When he sold its products in the USSR, they did not have hard currency and he bartered for lady's shoes. These were so old fashioned in style, that he would never get anywhere with these in the west, but in Hungary, he could barter these for money and in each of the Balkan countries, he made friends, because he was able to pick up enough of these foreign languages to have conversations. In the process, he was invited to stay with the families of these newfound friends, who in turn gave him gifts, he was to display in his home for years to come. His proudest moment was, when one of his daughters, as Captain of the National Women's hockey team, won the gold in the Olympics in Los Angeles. This too was an inherited talent, as my mother won a prize in 1916 playing woman's field hockey.

Rudolf visited his brother one Sunday morning, wearing a jacket of an unusually beautiful colour brown and Jaap remarked that he liked to try to get one himself, and Rudolf gave him address of the store from which he brought that garment. Jaap tried to get one, but it was not available, as only a small number in that colour had been made. When Rudolf died, they found a note in one of the pockets. "For Jaap, I hope, that you have more pleasure from this jacket than I ever had". A picture was taken at Christmas time, showing Jaap wearing that jacket. It is sad to know, that shortly thereafter, that jacket had to find yet another owner.

When we talk about reincarnation, we realize that due to our genes, that concept exists. When we look at our own children and see traits and talents, that we recognize our parents had, we see this as a form of reincarnation. In our case, since the talents and traits of both our parents were similar, this is twice as remarkable with them. Often physical aspects of our lives are also inherited and that is not always positive. But if we are prone to heart problems, for instance and this is clearly inherited from our parents, the medical advances in the past years are so enormous, that our chances of survival are so much better than our parents'. In their last years they were very well cared for and we are thankful for that. They lived in another century, and ours is different. We have to attend to our own problems in ours' as well, but they gave us all the traits and talents, to give us a good life. Our problems might be different, but if our parents were able to live under the German occupation for five years, surely, we can handle, what is coming our way. My brothers are lost, but we still have our memories and photographic images to remind us of the years they were part of our lives. I sure miss them.

CHAPTER THIRTY

EXILE

We were on a day trip with Alan one day, who is a real estate appraiser. He had to travel to the Northern part of the province to appraise Roman Catholic churches in villages and towns for fire insurance purposes. We marveled at how large some churches were in remote areas, and how some churches in small villages had so many beautiful stained windows. At the end of the day, he wanted to visit one more church on the list, but it was getting dark and we wondered if he had to come back another day, because he had to make pictures outside of the church with his digital camera and it was probably too dark already to be successful.

On our return, he went to his computer to check how the pictures turned out and all we saw was that the last pictures were almost black. "Do you have to go back up North again?" we asked. "Not likely", he answered and started to push some buttons. "You see, the camera picked up the images and they are all in there. I just have to manipulate my computer a bit", and sure enough, within minutes, we saw the church, green grass, some trees and flowers along the driveway'. I was thinking of that day, because, when disaster struck in our lives, all we seem to notice is one big black picture. But a better image is still in there and all we have to do is to push a few buttons.

Our home in Stoneycroft was built in 1975 and the owner had built the house for his own family. Before this one, he built a house next door and while he was a good carpenter, he had financial problems. The ground around the house was a mess and it still looked like a building site. He never had the chance to enjoy his handy work, because when he received a big bill for building materials, with a letter indicating: "Pay up, or else", a real estate agent had to put a For Sale sign in front of the house. At the same time, we were driving past the house on a Sunday afternoon, looking for a more suitable home, because we lived in the country in a two-story house, which had become very difficult, having one child in a wheel chair.

We stopped and asked the salesman if we could have a look inside. He let us in and when Lydie saw the massive open fireplace made of large gray stones, and the cedar ceilings in the living room and hall, we told him that we were prepared to make an offer right then and there. But he refused, because it was Sunday and then we wanted to know, when he was in his office next day and at the time he told us we were in his office. That was when we bought the house. We asked the lawyer if there were any leans on the property and he said no, and if there were, he would be responsible for payment. As it turned out he had to eat his words and pay an overdue property tax bill.

We landscaped the grounds around the house and decided not to cut any trees unless they were dead, with the result, that we have the most trees in the neighbourhood, on our property and hundreds of birds, raccoons and deer are regular visitors. One year we saw a small story in the paper about a Federal Government grant program, that would pay one third of the cost of a renovation if we could show that energy saving would result because of that project. We built a sunroom with big windows on the south side of the house, just by extending the roofline and we received a cheque for four thousand dollars. Friends, hearing about it, made applications as well, but found out that the program had a short lifespan, as the Government did not expect so many applications.

In the summer of 2003, we noticed water drops coming down the walls in the living room and since the cedar ceiling was stained, it left brown streaks all over the walls. Alan knew a very reliable contractor, who had renovated his kitchen and he asked him to have a look. He told us that he could only find out what the problem was by taking down part of the ceiling, and we asked him reluctantly, to do what needed to be done. After an extensive inspection, the verdict was in: The whole roof had to be taken off the house, after which a whole new roof would be built. All the beams were rotten and all the electric wiring was so bad, it caused shorts. We moved all the furniture to the sunroom and then the contractor told us that the health department would not allow us to live in our home while it was in this condition.

Alan and Janet invited us to stay at their home and the contractor went to work with his son and a helper. We contracted an engineering firm to do an inspection and to give recommendations to the contractor, just in case he would miss something. Alan used all his expertise to make the best decisions necessary and because of his connections, new rafters, new doors, new light fixtures and trim for the rooms were bought, because he felt, that while we were doing the roof, we might as well renovate other parts of the house to keep in step with new construction developments and the times.

Now another problem arose which came with some wonderful side effects. We were still living at Alan and Janet's home and occupied a bedroom there. Then we learned that Flory and her daughter Caro were coming over to celebrate with us our 50th Wedding Anniversary. We felt, that they needed a couple of rooms, and we would stay in a local hotel for that week. When we told Alan and Janet, they told us that we would go to a large Bed and Breakfast in a mansion up the street, as a matter of fact, they already had reserved a room for us, and actually had paid the bill in advance. We had a marvelous week with an open house and Janet had everything ready for the guests. We had a family dinner in a nice restaurant, we ourselves had arranged and we almost forgot our problems at home.

Now the furniture in the sunroom had to be moved to Glenn's double garage, but he had sold the house and moved in with Alan and Janet as well. Then Patrick came over from Hamilton, Ontario to be at the festivities and he stayed in the computer room. Apparently, Glenn had arranged with the new owners that he could borrow the garage for a while as our furniture was safe there. After that week we held a painting party and a large number of friends came over on a Saturday, to paint the rooms of our house. Then shortly before Christmas we were able to bring the furniture back and again move back in our house. Now Glenn moved temporarily in with us. He put hardwood flooring in two rooms and now our home looked like new and inviting. At first we looked at a disaster, but soon we realized that when everything was done, we had a much more comfortable home.

CHAPTER THIRTY-ONE

CHANGE OF HEART

On Halloween, October 31st 2006, we were both going to a Kiwanis luncheon, where a local historian was going to tell stories about ghosts in the city. On our way, Lydie made one pit stop at the family doctors' office, and since it was going to be a short visit, I waited in the car. After ten minutes waiting, she came into the car and told me that all plans were off, as the doctor had discovered a heart murmur, and she had to report herself to the emergency department of the Saint John Regional Hospital. There she was hooked on to all kind of machines, an X-Ray machine was wheeled-in and they took some blood. She learned that she had to be admitted and at suppertime, she was in her room, where she stayed for seven days.

Lydie was on the waiting list for double by-pass surgery to repair a heart valve and she was told that the intention was to do that within a month. She returned home to wait her turn, but after three days, she woke up in the middle of the night, was sitting straight up in bed and had breathing problems. She did not sleep a wink. We drove to the hospital and within fifteen minutes she was back in emergency department again. At around five o'clock, she moved upstairs, back into the same room with the fabulous view. Glenn and I were visiting when the surgeon came in. The surgeon told us that one artery was totally blocked and another artery was blocked by 80%.

Since one valve was leaking badly, he was going to try to repair it. When asked about the risk involved, he indicated that the risk of failure in her case was between 3 and 5%. The operation, however, was a success and Lydie stayed in intensive care for one day. She was moved to a room with six patients for observation for one night and then moved to her private room. Doctors wanted her to walk right away and after five days she could go home. They gave her a small red pillow for protection of the breastbone area and told her that she was not to push nor pull anything. Others had to open doors for her.

When she went home, she was given a metal suitcase containing a video. Every morning, as she was hooked up to the videophone, a nurse would call her, and vital information was sent over the phone line to the hospital's computer. Using the camera on the videophone, the nurse asked Lydie to show the incision area. The Extra Mural nurse would come by next morning to change bandages. This system was a local innovation by the staff of the hospital, which received a National prize for the innovation, and now other hospitals are copying their system. The hospital does 800 of these operations each year and they are very successful. Included in the after care program is ten weeks of a full rehabilitation program in the hospital, which consists of consults with dietitians, physiotherapists and other professionals, and a session in the gym on exercise machines. Every Monday and Wednesday afternoon, for about three hours, she was rejuvenated by exercise, and within weeks, she was rehabilitated. In the process she had a new lease on life.

CHAPTER THIRTY-TWO

LIFE IS CHANGING

Patrick was in his second year at college, studying to be a youth counselor it was 2008 and he was doing great. His marks were very high, and when he had to do practical work at a group home or institution, he showed that he was going to be perfect for this career. At the end of the year he was getting his diploma at the Trade and Convention Centre in Saint John and he certainly would graduate with honors. But life is not always what we expect.

In the spring, changes in Patrick's life would prove to affect the lives of the whole family. When he was at his dentist for a possible tooth infection, the dentist pulled a tooth or molar and discovered something suspicious. A specialized dental surgeon was consulted and after a biopsy was taken, it was discovered that Patrick had cancer in his jawbone. After week's stay in hospital, Patrick was sent to Halifax to have surgery. Glenn had an appointment to have knee surgery during the same week, so Lydie and I took Patrick to Halifax. We stayed for a week at Pleasant Point Lodge, which is a nine-storey building, which provides accommodation for families who have a family member in the hospital. We learned that Patrick's cancer occurs mostly in children and only one in three million adults, it was recommended that he should receive chemotherapy and radiation treatments, both which could be given in Saint John.

Patrick went back to Saint John, and after a while it was decided that the radiation had to be carried out in Halifax, because that particular hospital was more advanced in treating patients in very delicate areas of the body. Radiation treatment was to be carried out for seven weeks and he was to report at the hospital daily for chemo regularly. Meanwhile, Glenn's surgery was successful, and after a while, Glenn returned to Halifax to be with Patrick. Luckily, we were available to help Glenn with Patrick's needs. Glenn needed assistance and friends were always ready to help. The hospital arranged for Glenn to stay close to Patrick when he was in hospital, either in the lodge, or at the Mennonite home. Both places provided Glenn with a home away from home.

We went to Halifax and stayed with the daughter of friends of ours who lived twenty minutes from the hospital on the other side of the river. We visited Patrick in the hospital twice every day. Patrick's room at the Lodge was kept open for him during his five-day hospital stay. Everything seemed to go as planned. Patrick, however, had some setbacks, which were immediately attended to. Again, he had many friends visiting him.

J.D. was a friend of the family who was a pilot in the air force. After he retired, he was hired by a commercial airline as a pilot. J.D. visited Patrick during his stay in Halifax and gave him the last medal he received from the air force. Patrick was overwhelmed with pleasure and gratitude, and that gave Patrick a real boost. The nurses loved Patrick and he knew each one by their first name. Patrick gave the nurses a real boost, which they could well use, because the department where they worked didn't give then too many chances to smile. We noticed that sometimes they just entered the room with any excuse, just to talk to him.

Things can change in minutes. Glenn and Patrick returned home from Halifax one particular Monday. As soon as they arrived home, Glenn's cell phone rang. They were told by the hospital in Halifax that Patrick had to be admitted on Thursday for surgery on the following Monday. Three surgeons would be involved and Glenn would stay the previous night in a cot in his room. He hardly slept that night. After the surgery, we would again make the trip to Halifax and stay there for a while. The surgeons operated for over ten hours. During the proceedings they made many photographs to study and help many other patients in the future.

When this began, he suggested that this experience, in the end, would help him in his work by understanding children with serious problems. What he called the "fight of his life" when he was diagnosed, was a fight he felt he had won, by showing how much courage he could muster. He clearly takes after his father. Glenn has showed a great deal of courage himself during his life so far. We were not the only people who thought like that. In an e-mail of a friend of the family, we read: "Give our love to Patrick and tell him how totally amazed we are with his courage and spirit. He has set an example for all, with his grit and determination. Now is the time for everyone to rest and recuperate". It is obvious that our thumbs were up for him as well. In November he would get his diploma and, with his marks now in the 90%, he would have a bright future. But life is not always what we expect.

Yet another roadblock was coming our way. It was at the beginning of October, two weeks after the operation, and Patrick was coming home. Now a recuperation period was beginning in earnest. Alan had the town house cleaned from top to bottom, and we brought a container with fall flowers. We were glad the ordeal of over half a year, was over. By mid October Glenn and Patrick returned to Halifax to hear from the surgeons that the cancer was all gone. Before leaving, the head surgeon told them that he was confident that he had indeed removed all of the cancer. Patrick had planned his future and he studied hard for two years. Even during his illness, he wrote his final essays and he was at the top of his class. Unfortunately Patrick was going to miss his graduation ceremony at the Trade and Convention Centre, but he was ready to counsel troubled youths. But that too was not going to happen either.

Although we were confident that he was on the mend, some cancer cells had migrated to other parts of his body and now he was too weak to receive radiation. Shortly thereafter he was sent to the palliative care unit, and within two weeks he died in his sleep.

Patrick made his mark in the world and the hundreds of very good friends that attended his funeral showed that his life was all about giving. He planned to make his mark in social work, but that was not to be. He always thought of helping others, even when he was still in school. In his short life he traveled more than most people, all throughout North America and the Netherlands, the country of his grandparents. He traveled with his dad and with Brian, whose life was cut short as well. Seven hundred people came to attend his funeral, to show how much he was loved and admired. There were many people we did not even know, and many told us stories about him we were never aware of.

One visitor told us that once, Patrick found a teenager living in the streets, he took him to his apartment, washed him, fed him and made some phone calls to help him. He even gave him some of his clothes. He had many very good friends; one of which came over from British Columbia for the funeral. There were so many cards, flowers, phone calls from overseas, and e-mails were arriving daily, that it took days to answer all of them. A personal letter from the Premier of the Province of New Brunswick was a surprise, as was a leather folio with a printed proclamation by a Provincial Cabinet Minister living in our town, who proclaimed in the New Brunswick Legislature that Patrick had passed away. This was surprising to us because our province is larger that the Netherlands but has only 750,000 citizens, surely they would not do that for everyone? Was it because of his tender age, or how he dealt with other people? Nobody will know.

When our kids grew up, we instilled, by example, the need for them to look after each other, and they did just that. When our son Brian became wheelchair bound, we cared for him until it was impossible for us to lift him in and out of bed. Glenn took over and looked after him for eight years, and this damaged his knees, and his knee eventually had to be replaced. When his own son became ill with cancer, he looked after him for over eight months, day and night at home, and even in the hospital. Alan and Janet too were always very supportive to Alan's brothers. Support also came from his many friends who were always ready to help at the drop of a hat. Patrick supportive friends included both seniors and kids.

Patrick seems to have done more in his twenty six years than most of us and of all the friends who stood by Glenn and Patrick, one stands out. April deWolfe was with Patrick in Halifax and in Saint John almost constantly, taking charge when Glenn was exhausted and in need of support, and she was helping Patrick whenever possible. With her own kids at home, that was a tall order, but she managed. She owned a home in the country and Glenn, not being a city person himself, saw his whole life change into something he always longed for. Glenn came to admire her and then love her and during the spring he started to share his life with her and they were married outside their home and just close family members were present to wish them well. Now, together with an instant family, they continue on their own unpredictable and unexpected journey.

LIFE CONSISTS NOT IN HOLDING GOOD CARDS,
BUT IN PLAYING WELL THOSE YOU HOLD __

JOSH BILLINGS

PEOPLE MENTIONED IN THIS STORY

Arnold Carl von Weiler (1882-1993)
And Isabella von Weiler (van Styrum) 1887-1969)

Their Children:

Joost Robert von Weiler (1926-)
    Married to Lydie Hilbertine Annie van der Kolk (1928-)

Florentine Adrienne von Weiler (Bok) (1917-)

Jacob Willem von Weiler (1919-2001)
    Married to Mathilde Amelie Gunning (1919-2003)

Carl Rudolf Theodoor von Weiler (1928-2001)
    Married to Adelia Diliana Cornelia Maria van Eysden (1933-1986)
    and Martine Verburgh Kwindt

Children of Joost and Lydie:

Alan John von Weiler (1955-)
    Married to: Janet Macdonald (1958-)
    Daughter Lisa Marlene von Weiler (1979-)
    Married to Timothy Nichols
    Son: Sebastian Xavier Morrow (2001-)

Brian Rudolph von Weiler (1956-1997)

Glenn Gerald von Weiler (1961-)
    Son: Patrick Alexander Brian von Weiler (1982-2008)

Other , not family:

Jacob Lambert Wilhelm Carl von Weiler (1902-1938)
    Inventor, naval officer, university professor ("Radarman")

Judge Rodman E. Logan, QC

Lieutenant Carleton and York Regiment,
Provincial Court Judge, New Brunswick Court of Queen's Bench.

Prince Bertil of Sweden.
His passion was automobiles and he was a promoter of Swedish
products with modern designs.

Lord Provost of Edinburgh Sir Myer Galpern

Peter Gzowsky
Broadcaster, editor, reporter, named "The Voice of Canada"

Stephen Mezei,
Author, scriptwriter and instructor of the Arts at York University

John Robert Columbo,
Author, anthologist, Canadian poet, editor, essayist,
Humorist, author of many books.

Dora de Pedery-Hunt,
Hungarian born sculptor and designer of coinage bearing the portrait
of Queen Elizabeth II; she sculpted many commemorative medals
and internationally known.